CHASING DAYBREAK

BY RANAE GLASS

THIS book is a work of fiction. Names, characters, places and incidents are the product of the authors' imagination or are used factiously. Any resemblance to actual persons, living or dead, business establishments, events or locales is entirely coincidental.

Chasing Daybreak
Copyright ©2014 Ranae Glass
All rights reserved.
Cover Design by: Marya Heiman
Typography by: Courtney Nuckels

ISBN: 978-1-63422-033-0

For Tammy, Lisa, Dee Dee, Robin, and Patti.
The unstoppable Cothren sisters.
Love you to the moon and back!

CHAPTER 1

I cussed under my breath as the ropes binding my wrists tore at my raw flesh. The closet was dark, except for the flickering light beneath the door. Rancid-smelling smoke assaulted my nose and singed my throat, which was already raw from screaming. I bucked wildly against my restraints, fighting against the panic trying to seep into my brain.

Shane lay across from me in a crumpled heap, still unconscious from the dart full of animal tranquilizers the arsonist had hit him with. I had to admit, I was impressed. It took skill and planning to take down a vampire, even a newbie like Shane. As he slumped in the corner with his thin face slack, I watched his eyes moving restlessly behind their lids and wondered if he was dreaming. Could the dead dream? And if so, what did they dream about?

I didn't have to see his eyes to remember their exact shade of blue; I didn't have to hear him talk to remember the exact timbre of his voice. These things were burned into my mind, scars written across my heart that would never fade. As I grew old and time stole away all my other memories, those would remain. Seeing him lying there, looking so completely helpless, only fueled my slowly rising panic.

Despite my yelling and kicking, he lay useless in the corner of the closet as the house blazed around us. I sucked in a deep breath, trying to calm the frantic pulse of my heart. It was beating so loudly that it drowned out all other sound.

It was my second mistake of the day.

Immediately, I coughed and gagged, places deep in my stomach clenching against the scorching hot air. The Victorian house was burning, hot and fast like dry tinder.

We'd been hired by one seriously ticked-off landlord to investigate the mysterious infernos that had left the fire investigator scratching his head. He'd been stumped by both the intensity and apparent lack of accelerant. We discovered quickly—well, in fairness, Shane had discovered quickly—the source of the problem. The arsonist was using the one thing that would burn faster and hotter than gas, kerosene, or propane. Vampire blood. You didn't even need a match, just a little direct sunlight and... whoosh. Instant firebomb.

Not exactly an easy thing to get your hands on, vampire blood. The daylight-challenged folks tended to eat people who poked at them with sharp things—go figure. We'd narrowed it down to the handful of workers in the hospital's blood bank— the ones who had direct access to the vampire donors—and the rest was easy.

Well, maybe not exactly easy.

Recently divorced and fired from his job at the hospital weeks prior for tampering with the donations, Billy Young might as well have had a bull's eye painted on his forehead. Depressed, angry, and abused as a child, Young had decided to re-visit his own misery on the foster homes he'd lived in as a child. Once we were able to connect him to the houses, everything fell into place.

I never thought he'd be here today, never imagined we'd catch him in the act. And I sure as hell never figured he could take on Shane.

That was my first mistake.

Now I was trapped in a closet in a burning house with a living corpse and my hands tied behind my back.

Great. Just another relaxing Sunday afternoon.

Yet, ironically, it still wasn't the worst day of my life. Hell, it wasn't my worst day this month.

I wedged my back against the wall and kicked out with my legs. The door held fast. Stupid early Colonial construction. These houses were built like Sherman tanks.

"Shane Brooks, you wake up, you stupid, useless, unreliable vampire!" I tried to scream, but it came out in a strangled whisper. Smoke burned my eyes and tears streamed down my face from the acrid air.

Frantically, I rummaged around the bottom of the closet for something—anything—I could use to free my hands. The corner of the carpet had been torn up, exposing a long, jagged, tack strip. If there was one thing that could wake even a tranqued vamp, it was the smell of blood. The question

3

was—would being locked in a closet with a groggy, drugged, possibly hungry vampire be better than being locked in the closet with a useless, sleeping one? Crap. I hated having to choose between the lesser of two evils. Holding my breath, I pushed my hands down onto the rusty tacks. The pain was sharp and immediate.

Wonderful, I thought, adding the need for a tetanus shot to my 'stuff to do if I make it out of this alive' list. Right below take a shower and right above get my French manicure repaired.

I wiggled until my back was to Shane and squeezed my hands together, making the blood flow freely down my fingers. I'd always been good at bleeding, at least according to the way-too-chipper brunette at the donation van. I'd just never figured it would come in handy. Silly me.

I managed to flop onto my stomach on the floor. Shane lunged awake, his icy hands tearing at my restraints. I heard the snap before I felt it, before the circulation started to return, bringing with it the stinging needles of pain from the puncture wounds and the return of circulation.

Flipping swiftly onto my back, I prepared to brace my feet against his chest to fend off the coming attack—like I had any hope of holding my own against him. As it turned out, the maneuver was unnecessary. Shane shook his head and blinked rapidly. Hints of color returned to his cheeks.

"Are you all right, Isabel?" he asked after a second.

I sighed, part in relief, part in exasperation. The concern in his voice rang through my body,

4

reminding me of the person he'd been before he died.

I was taken with another fit of coughing, and then gasped, "Just get us out of here, okay?"

Shane stood, utilizing his large frame to push open the closet door. It ripped off the hinges like it was made of tissue paper rather than solid oak.

The heat of the fire hit us full force, pushing us back into the closet. With my arm raised in front of me, I could barely see the layout of the room through the gray smoke. As my eyes adjusted to the intense light, pieces of falling timbers hit the floor a few feet in front of us. Shane let out a long, unnatural hiss as glowing red embers fell from the ceiling like aberrant snow.

The room was blazing from the bed to the curtains, the flames licking all the way to the ceiling, melting and bubbling the green plaster walls. I looked at Shane, who now cowered behind me. I knew that a single touch of those flames to his skin would send him up like a Roman candle. It wasn't just his blood that was flammable.

"Go, Isabel," he commanded, sensing my indecision.

Shane should have known me better than to even suggest it. Our relationship might not be all puppies and kittens, but he was my partner and there was no way I was going to leave without him. I turned to tell him as much, my hands already on my hips, when behind him, I saw the answer to our problems. Shoving him to the side, I tugged a massive, wheeled suitcase down from the shelf overhead. It was the size of a steamer trunk, only with soft sides and wheels on one edge.

I unzipped the case. "Get in!"

He threw me a disgusted look. "No."

"You got a better idea?" I snapped.

He climbed backward into the cramped case, pulling his knees tight into his chest, and sighed heavily.

I struggled to get the zipper started. "Time to lay off the carbs, Shane."

He snorted and exhaled a deep breath, shrinking further into the faux-leather bag. Finally, the zipper groaned and gave way, beginning its journey around the track. It got stuck in the corner, forcing me to push hard on Shane's bulging shoulder.

"Ouch!"

"Oh, shut up! You're dead for shit's sake. Suck it up!"

Baggage securely zipped, I pulled up the handle and ran from the closet, only to be immediately assaulted by the noxious fumes, the thick smoke obscuring my vision. I leaned into the doorjamb, swiping my sleeve across my face to sop up some of the sweat and tears in my eyes, struggling to make sense of the scene around me.

With my decision made, I managed to tug the case into the hallway. We were upstairs, but the front door was visible from the top step and, luckily, it was relatively clear of flames. How long that would remain true was another story. I launched myself down the narrow stairs, the heavy suitcase banging down the steps behind me. I have to admit, the mental picture of Shane in that tumbling bag made me smile just a little.

I was almost to the last step when the stairs gave way. Flames crawled up from beneath the shards of wood, threatening to engulf me—and my baggage. With an enormous heave, I freed myself from the debris and pulled the relatively undamaged suitcase off the burning rubble. Just as I reached for the door, it flew open, hitting my outstretched arm and sending me sprawling across the parquet floor.

Standing in the doorway, looking slightly confused, was a fireman in a bulky, yellow suit. Seeing me, he scooped me into his arms and turned for the door. I screamed and hit him on the back, trying to make myself understood over the chaos. I pointed frantically at the case on the floor, but he shook his head and continued to try to get me out the door. Now I was being thoroughly uncooperative, clutching the doorjamb with both hands, even as my wounded arm screamed in protest. The maneuver must have been unexpected because I fell free of his arms and crawled to the case before he could reach me.

"My partner is in there," I screamed repeatedly.

Finally, he seemed to understand and, helping me to my feet, tugged me and my heavy baggage into the yard where police and paramedics waited.

Soon, I was sitting in the back of an ambulance, sucking oxygen through a plastic mask while trying to explain the situation to a sympathetic-looking EMT. Across the yard, a curious patrol officer unzipped the suitcase and Shane burst out. His eyes were red with panic, his skin opalescent in the reflection of the flames. The orange glow from behind illuminated him harshly, making him look like a demon. Or, more accurately, he looked like what he was, a monster.

In a flash, a dozen cops were commanding him to lie on his stomach with his hands clasped behind his head. He obeyed slowly, realizing he was locked in their crosshairs. I rolled my eyes.

"Here we go again," I muttered.

CHAPTER 2

Back at the station, Chief Haynes stared at me over the rim of his well-used coffee mug. I was still wearing the scratchy, gray blanket the EMTs had nestled around my shoulders, as if the thin cloth would hold the hysteria of a five-foot three-inch woman at bay. Shane hadn't been so lucky. After reluctantly allowing himself to be handcuffed, he was tossed in the back of a squad car and brought in for questioning. Only my vouching for him had kept him out of the dank basement cell they reserved for their plasma-challenged guests. *As if metal bars would have held a vampire anyway*, I thought dryly.

"Vampire blood?" Chief Haynes repeated as if the words were completely alien to his mouth. I should have expected this. Vampires had only been out of the coffin for a few years, and most local authorities had no idea what to do with the information. They weren't citizens yet, legally anyway, and they weren't really people. That put them in a gray spectrum for those people whose job it was to rush in and risk their lives for them.

I couldn't really blame them. I'd been living with a vampire in my attic for almost a year, and sometimes, I wanted to stake him myself.

Despite the residual quaking in my hands, I tried to stay professional. "As I explained earlier, the fire bug, Billy Young, was recently on staff at Victory General Hospital. We discovered he'd been stealing blood from the vampire blood unit. He was using it to destroy the homes he'd lived in as a foster child," I explained.

I'd called the station as soon as we had Young's identity figured out and left a message for the chief. Shane and I had only gone to that particular house to try to confirm what Young was using as accelerant but, as my run of bad luck was holding this month, he'd still been in the house when we got there.

I was eager to go home and take a hot bath, to wash off the ash, sweat, and fear that clung to my skin like dry glue. I was equally eager to see what they'd done with Shane. While I was on my way with the chief to give my statement at the station, the local cops had decided to 'question' Shane. If you asked me, he was extremely lucky some trigger-happy cop hadn't put a few holes in him at the scene, just for good measure.

Of course, regular bullets wouldn't have really hurt him. They just would have pissed him off.

Haynes nodded. "Yeah. The staties caught up with Young at the Battery. He was about to blow his own head off, dumb son of a..."

I coughed, not because Haynes was about to injure my delicate female sensibilities with his language, but because I had probably just inhaled enough soot to make up for a lifetime of not smoking.

"Your, err, partner, Shane, is waiting outside to drive you home." He motioned to the door and stood. "Thanks for getting to the bottom of this. I never would have thought..."

I shook his hand and practically bounded out the door. Shane was standing rigidly against the wall of chairs near the entrance. He saw me and motioned for me to take his arm. I considered refusing, but after the time he'd surely had with the police, I figured he could use a show of support, no matter how small.

Maybe we didn't always get along, but we always had each other's backs.

By the time we got home, it was nearly dawn. Shane said a quick good night and bolted up to his room. If anything untoward had happened back at the station, he didn't say anything about it and I didn't ask.

I tossed my purse and keys into the worn, orange chair in the living room. It was one of the many throwbacks littering the place, remnants of my father, which I couldn't bring myself to part with, no matter how hideous. The house was old before the turn of the century, nestled near the Charleston University campus. Dad's shingle still hung beside the black iron mailbox affixed beside the front door. *Stone Investigations.* Once a respectable PI, he'd earned a reputation for being willing to take on any case, from following and filming elicit affairs, to helping the city's vamps track down long-forgotten blood relatives.

The attic had been converted into a dark room back when my father took over the detective agency from his father some thirty-odd years ago. Back before the age of digital photography, my father had carefully developed all his own photos in there. Now, the darkroom served as perfect sleeping quarters for my photosensitive buddy. When he moved in, we'd rearranged a few things, put in a small bed, and a phone. I'd offered to put in a small bathroom, but he curtly informed me that vampires didn't need to pee. *Ever.*

Which was way more than I needed to know.

He did, however, make up for it by taking the longest showers in the history of ever in the downstairs bathroom, more often than not leaving me to wake up to an ice bath.

When Dad passed away early last year, the business and the house fell to me. I was the oldest of four daughters—which was a continual disappointment to my father who, despite his affection for his girls, always dreamed of having a son to pass the business on to. When he had the first heart attack two summers ago, he called me home from college and gave me the rundown of our family's legacy, and my responsibilities to keep it afloat.

Of course, I never really thought he was going to die. I expected, however irrationally, that he would be around forever. So even as Dad was preparing me for the job, I still figured I'd get my teaching degree, settle down, get married, and have a life of my own.

When he died the next year, I reluctantly left

school permanently and came home to run the office.

I'd be the first to admit I had no real desire to be a PI, but as it turned out, my natural curiosity and nosiness made me well suited for it.

The office had originally been my great-grandparents' home, but as the family grew, they needed more space, so they eventually moved into a larger house on the outskirts of the city. The business had remained in the old house. Now it was mine.

The only full bath in the house was on the second floor, complete with a new Jacuzzi tub I'd forced Shane to help me install. Running the water as hot as I could stand it, I stepped in, allowing the rushing jets to massage out the kinks in my neck and back. There were ugly rope burns on my wrists, as well as cuts on both hands, and multiple red welts that would bruise by tomorrow. *Great.* I hated having to wear long sleeves in the heat of summer, but it was better than the alternative, which was looking like a leper.

Tomorrow, I had to make my weekly visit to my mother's bakery to give her a check from the office's meager account for my younger sister Sarah's tuition. Sarah was studying at UCLA, and the bakery barely paid for itself. I wasn't bitter about it or anything. To my surprise, I enjoyed running the agency. After my personal life had fallen apart, it was a refuge, a haven for me, and later, for Shane, too. Days like today, however, made me wish I'd become something safer, like an astronaut or a ninja.

I also had a meeting tomorrow—*strike that*, I thought weakly, *tonight*—with a prospective new client. From the initial conversation, it sounded like he wanted us to find his missing daughter. I relaxed deeper into the water, adding a splash of lavender oil for my dry skin. It stung my wounds for only a second before filling the room with a soft, sweet scent.

It would be a nice change of pace to work on a human case for once, I thought weakly.

It seemed like all we did anymore was supernatural crap. As soon as people got word I'd brought a vamp on as a partner, they started coming out of the woodwork with bizarre requests. One lady wanted us to prove her husband was turning into a werewolf once a month. Better that than admit he was probably having an affair, which he was. Unfortunately, we'd had several legitimate paranormal cases, too. There was a family whose teenage daughter was sneaking out at night to see her teenage-looking boyfriend. Luckily, the vamp was over three hundred years old, and we got to turn that one over to the DA as a case of statutory rape. His punishment had yet to be decided, but he was sure staying the hell away from sixteen-year-old girls. For now, anyway. The courts were arguing between sending the pedi-vamp to some sort of dark hole for a few months or just killing him. Of course, he'd been changed in his mid-thirties. I couldn't help but wonder if it might have been different if he'd been turned as a teenager himself. It'd be interesting to see what the courts had to say about that.

At some point during my mental volley regarding vampire law, I dozed off in the tub.

What woke me was the temperature drop. My teeth were chattering so hard I thought they might crack, my skin ridged like a basketball with all the goose bumps. Sloshing the now-cold water over the edge of the tub, I stepped out and wrapped myself in a large, white towel. As I headed to my room, I peeked down the stairs to see rays of morning sun streaming in the downstairs windows. Releasing a heartfelt sigh, I climbed into the warm blankets of my bed and fell back into blissful oblivion.

CHAPTER 3

The buzzing alarm startled me out of unconsciousness. I slapped the "off" button, making a mental note to kick the shit out of the guy who'd locked me in that damn closet the night before—that was, if the cops didn't take care of the job first. Not only was I running on about four hours of sleep, but also my bruises were throbbing and all my muscles were stiff and tight despite my hot soak.

Dressed in a modest gray pantsuit, I headed downstairs to get a cup of coffee and prepare for my first meeting. The nice thing about having a home office was that most days I could work in pajama pants and bunny slippers if I wanted to—which was why I saw clients by appointment only. Today, however, there would be no such luxury for me.

It was just after eleven when Mr. Curtis arrived. I showed him to my office and closed the door behind us. Walking behind my desk, I slowly lowered myself into my desk chair, the muscles in my back protesting angrily. The still-warm mug of coffee in my hand helped.

"Can I get you anything?" I asked.

I'd wanted to hire a secretary or at least some sort of assistant for a while, but business had been slower than expected, and overhead had been higher. Most days, that left the job to Shane, but he was still snoozing so the schmoozing the clients was all me today.

It wasn't something I was particularly good at.

"No, thank you, Miss Stone. I'm fine."

Richard Curtis didn't look fine. His yellow polo shirt was wrinkled and his gray hair unruly. He had dark patches under his eyes, and the lines on his face were etched deep.

"Why don't you tell me how I can help you today?" I nudged.

He sat rigid in the tall, hard-back chair, his hands folded tightly in his lap. My voice must have been curt because he blinked at me like I'd reached out and slapped him.

I took a deep breath. "Sorry. I was out late on assignment last night, so I didn't get much sleep. I didn't mean to sound short. Please, tell me what you need."

My voice was much friendlier, and I even smiled. It still may not have seemed sincere, though. It was hard to act interested on four hours' sleep. I sat back and waited.

"You've heard about my daughter, Lisa Welch?"

I nodded. Everyone from Charleston to Tucson had seen the headlines or heard the news reports. Lisa Welch, thirty-one-year-old mother of four, local cheerleading coach, and church pianist had gone missing six months before. After an exhaustive search, all the police had found was her purse and her abandoned car at the local mall. Suspicion ran wild; search parties were formed, all with no success. It was as if she'd simply vanished into thin air.

"The police called off the investigation last week." His voice cracked, a mix of sadness, desperation, and anger. I sympathized.

"We'd be happy to look into the case, Mr. Curtis, but you should know, I can't make any promises. I'll call the local police and get a look at the case file, with your permission, but the police have vast resources and I'm sure they were quite thorough..."

He frowned. That wasn't what he wanted to hear, which was exactly why I had to say it. Grieving families wanted assurances, guarantees. Heck, they wanted miracles.

I wasn't in the miracle business.

"However," I continued, "we will do everything in our power to find your daughter."

He perked up, his hand sliding into his back pocket to produce a checkbook. Tossing the slim piece of leather on my desk, he picked up a pen.

"Money is no object, Miss Stone..."

I laid my hand over the booklet, closing it.

"I appreciate that, but why don't I take a look at the file, and make sure I'll be able to help you before we worry about payment?"

No reason to take this man's hard-earned cash unless I could actually do something besides read a file. My father had been the same way.

No wonder we weren't wealthy.

We stood. I moved around the desk to open the door and motion him toward the entryway door.

He turned, his hand on the knob, and looked at me with earnest, sad eyes.

"Your father was a good man. That's why I came to you with this. He'd be proud," Mr. Curtis said hoarsely before turning and walking into the hot summer afternoon.

"I hope so," I whispered to myself. "I hope so."

I watched Mr. Curtis drive away from my curb before closing the door. As soon as he was gone, I let out a yawn I'd been trying to hold back all morning. My body was at war with itself. Half of me begged for more sleep, the other half demanded nourishment. My growling stomach won out, and I locked up the office as I headed out to see my mother.

I arrived at the family bakery with one of Bubba Sly's famous Philly Cheese steaks in hand. It was the best deli in the state, and right around the corner from Mom's shop. I'd had no intentions of stopping at Bubba's—really—I hadn't, but the smell made my mouth water as I passed the front door. After a brief internal debate, my love of all things cheesy and steaky won out.

It was a typical Monday. The college kids were taking up every table at Mom's, munching on sandwiches and soup bowls between scribbling frantically in notebooks and reading lines of text. My mom saw the sandwich in my hand as soon as I walked in, making the overhead bell chime. She frowned at me.

She wasn't the first—even today.

I shrugged unapologetically and headed into the back office. Mom rung up the last customer in line before handing the register over to my sister, Phoebe, who had just finished busing an empty table.

Phoebe, only a year my junior, had dropped out of college in her first year and settled on a life as an amateur photographer, which I found ironic because people are always telling her she should be a model. She was beautiful, even in her old, cutoff shorts and a T-shirt. Phoebe had the long, wavy, brown hair that marked our Italian heritage. Her symmetrical features were accented with high cheekbones and full lips. Taller than I was, Phoebe had our mother's deep brown eyes.

Her life choices made Mom cringe in a 'what kind of respectable woman became a photographer?' way. As if there was something seedy about it, like she'd somehow become a trashy tabloid photographer or something. As it was, Phoebe worked mostly on the weekends doing weddings and such, leaving her free to help Mom out in the shop most days.

If it weren't for Phoebe working for tips and free cupcakes, the bakery would fold like a house of cards. It barely squeaked by as it was. The economic bust hit everyone hard. Folks that had been in business in Charleston for years were closing up shop. Even the college kids and tourists were cutting back wherever they could, which left a little business like Mom's in a financial pickle.

Two years ago, our youngest sister, Heather, had all but dropped off the face of the earth. At sixteen, she decided she needed to 'experience life' and had taken off to backpack across Europe. Now Mom got the occasional postcard and a note about whatever city Heather was squatting in and whatever loser guy she'd latched on to. She hadn't even bothered to come home for Dad's funeral.

We didn't talk about Heather.

"I heard you had some excitement last night," Mom muttered as she slumped down onto the old couch in her cramped office. I was in her desk chair, mouth full of food, so I just shrugged. This was how we communicated. She talked, and I half-paid attention. We'd been close once, but my recent situation had her fearing for my very soul. Ironically, it was only partly because I was playing house with the living dead. The main issue was the fact that, at twenty-two, I was nearly an old maid and didn't have a house full of obnoxious Italian children.

I swallowed loudly. "I came by to bring the check for Sarah's tuition this semester."

Sarah, barely nineteen and the spitting image of our father, was already in her second year of school thanks to a streak of severe overachieverness.

"I know." She sighed. "It's the only reason you come see me anymore. You should come by for dinner tonight. Frank Calontoni—you remember him, Stephanie's son from across the street—he's home from dental school this week. I'm sure we could have them over too..."

I gagged on my sandwich.

Frank, from middle school. I wondered for a moment if the eczema had cleared up, and then I shook my head.

"Can't, Ma. Shane and I have to go talk to Reggie down at the station tonight."

I hadn't actually set that up yet, but anything

was better than one of my mom's 'come and see my single daughter' dinners. I'd done it before and left feeling like an exhibit at a freak show. At the mention of Shane, she made a grunting sound low in her throat. Nothing raised her hackles like the mention of my one-time fiancé turned blood-sucking roomie.

"You'd think that today, of all days, you'd want to be away from that monster."

I wrinkled my brow. "Today?"

She sighed and pointed at her desk calendar. "Do you know what day it is?"

"Uh... June sixth..." *Oh.* I saw her point.

Today was the one-year anniversary of the day Shane had left me at the altar. Not that it was entirely his fault. He had been a smidge preoccupied, being attacked by a psycho vampire and all.

"I'm so over all that," I lied smoothly, still staring at the calendar on her cluttered desk as if it were an alien being.

She just gave me *that look*. You know, the one moms gave you when they knew you were completely and totally full of shit.

"And he's living in your attic *because*?"

I rolled my eyes. We'd been over this a million times.

Because he'd been attacked and turned into a blood-sucking demon. Because he'd been unable to go back to his job as a teacher afterward. Because the vamp that turned him and was supposed to take care of him had been hunted down and killed for creating him without the blessing of the local Vamp-in-Charge. He'd had no place else to go, and no one else to depend on. His own folks had cursed and spit on him when he tried to go home. I was all he had. Besides, a small, tiny, mutinous part of myself still loved him.

And I hated him for that.

The day Shane had been thrust back into my life was a turning point for me, for both of us really. Even though I'd been expecting him, the knock on my door had surprised me. I'd been drifting for days on the sensation that none of it was real, that at any moment I'd wake up to find it had all been a horrible dream.

When I'd answered the door, Shane stood there, in the cool, spring rain, water dripping off the tip of his nose. He had a duffle bag in one hand and a bag of blood in the other. His eyes were drawn to the ground as if he couldn't quite bring himself to look me in the eye. It shattered the fragile grip of sanity I'd been holding on to and I ran to him, throwing my arms around him as I had so many times before. I wanted him to hold me, to tell me everything was going to be all right. I never needed another human being so much in my life as I needed him in that moment. He wound his fingers in my hair. Dropping everything else at his feet, he crushed his mouth to mine and kissed me passionately, ferociously. I lost myself in him.

Until I felt the sharp prick of his fangs in my bottom lip. The taste of old pennies filled my mouth, making my stomach churn. I tried to pull away, but he held me tightly, his fingers digging into my skin, pulling my hair painfully. I screamed into his mouth and clawed at his face with my fingernails.

Finally, he dropped me, literally, into a puddle at his feet. Wiping my hand across my mouth, I smeared the blood that was still seeping from my lip. I looked into his eyes, expecting remorse, but I saw only cold, red eyes. He licked his lip hungrily. I backpedaled quickly across the threshold of the front door. He took a predatory step forward before regaining control of himself. Shaking his head, he blinked, his eyes returning to their natural hue. Using the door to brace myself, I stood, dripping onto the wood floor.

"I'll go," was all he said as he turned to leave.

"Go where?" I'd asked. Even then, he meant more to me than my own safety. The idea of him out in the world alone, scavenging like a stray dog, twisted knots in my heart.

He shrugged.

"Come in, Shane, please," I whispered shakily.

He turned, searching my face with his eyes.

"I can't be with you," he said finally. "I don't trust myself not to hurt you."

I wanted to reassure him, to tell him that none of it mattered. But deep down, I knew it would be a lie. Everything had changed. Nothing would ever be the same again.

"We can't go back, I know that. But maybe we can start something new. We can be friends," I offered, though it physically hurt to utter the words.

He nodded. "Friends."

He'd stepped inside my door, and we'd been working on the whole 'friends' thing ever since. It didn't erase the past. It didn't stop me from missing him. It was messy, complicated, and painful, but it worked when so few things in my life had.

"Here's the check, Ma." I stuffed it in her hands and scooped up the unfinished sandwich. "I gotta run."

Mom kissed me on the cheek as I practically launched myself out the door, waving quickly to Phoebe, the only daughter who still had the patience to listen to her lectures.

The shades were all drawn when I got back to the office, signaling Shane's presence downstairs. I opened the door slowly, letting as little light as possible into the house and flipping over the OPEN sign as I went. I found Shane in the kitchen, chugging a bag of A-positive straight from the fridge, making my newly full stomach lurch violently.

"Morning, Sleeping Ugly," I greeted him, trying to hide my revulsion as I strode in and sat down to look over the day's mail.

"Same to you." He gulped between sucking noises. My stomach rolled again, and I swallowed a gag.

"Anything good?" he asked, tossing the empty bag in the trash, finally done with his liquid breakfast.

"Bills, bills, and a Victoria's Secret catalog," I answered mechanically.

He snatched the magazine from my hands. "Mine."

I tossed the bills aside. "I had the meeting with Mr. Curtis today."

"How'd it go?" He flipped through the pages, whistling occasionally.

26

"I told him we'd go over the file. Try to find some new leads, see if the investigators overlooked anything."

"You think they did?" He was serious now, all business.

"I doubt it. But it's worth a fresh look. Maybe we can pick up on something. Either way, it's a place to start."

He opened his mouth to say something, but he was interrupted by the chime of the doorbell.

The UPS guy was there to drop off some packages. He glared at me as I signed on the electronic clipboard. He'd left one too many of my packages in the rain, and I'd finally called to complain to his boss. I wasn't sure what came of it, only that we now exchanged angry looks whenever forced to interact.

I scooped up the boxes and headed back inside, slamming the door with my foot. Setting them carefully on the kitchen counter, I turned and pulled a knife from a drawer. Cutting the tape made me feel like a kid at Christmas. Even if I ordered them myself, getting packages was one of my favorite things.

The first box fell open, showering packing peanuts on the floor as I pulled out my shiny, new night-vision camera. It was actually a combination of night vision and thermal, so it could take video in the dark with no light and read heat signatures through walls. I felt like James fucking Bond just holding it.

"This would have been helpful last night," I grumbled to myself.

"Hold up. I'm sleeping on the twin bed you had when you were fourteen, and yet you can afford these?" Shane complained.

I shot him a challenging glance. "If you don't like the bed, I'll just take it out and put in a nice, roomy coffin for you..."

He shuddered. Claustrophobia, apparently, was not one of the things you got over after becoming a vampire. Without another word, he pulled open the next box, revealing a plethora of goodies.

"What's all this?" he asked, licking the last drop of liquid from the corner of his mouth.

I pointed. "Bionic ear. Computer snooper. And micro-UHF room transmitter."

"Okay, this time in English."

I sighed, "This one lets us hear from distances of eighty yards, this one records and transmits keystrokes on a computer, and this one is a listening device."

"I don't know why you need this stuff. I'm better than any techno-gizmo," he bragged. "And I can hear way farther than eighty yards."

He was right. Shane was better than any gear I could buy, but the rational part of me knew I couldn't count on him being around forever.

"Yeah, well, you know, in case you die for real next time..."

He thought about that for a minute before responding, "I'd just come back and haunt you."

"Funny, I thought you already were," I said earnestly.

"Nah. If I were a ghost, you couldn't make me clean the dishes."

I raised an eyebrow. "You wanna bet?"

The rest of the afternoon passed with me at the computer paging through the articles and coverage of the Welch disappearance. There was a lot of media speculation, but no real leads. Shane sat behind me, making notes as I read aloud.

"Lisa Welch disappeared from her home in Summerville on January 14th of this year. The neighbors reported nothing unusual, at least not to the press. Her four kids were in school, husband at work. That's about it. It talks a little about her charity work, nothing helpful. Did you call Reggie?"

Reggie Lukas was the lead detective on the case, and an old family friend. He was also one of the few people in town who treated Shane like he was still a person and not some demon sent to steal their souls. His wife, Connie, had even invited Shane to dinner last month.

The older vamps in town pretty much ignored Shane, as he had no wealth or status, so it was good for him to feel like he belonged somewhere. I wondered if he'd change much when the vampire community really started to accept him. I kind of hoped not.

"Yeah, he said we can come down at six."

I stretched in my chair, "What time is it now?"

"Four-thirty. You need some food?"

I shook my head, "Nah, I'll grab something after."

"You know," he said with mock earnestness, "you really should lay off those fast food stops. They go right to your thighs."

I spun the chair and stared him down. "My foot

is going to go right to your ass here in a minute."

"Brave talk for a walking Happy Meal."

"Speaking of your repugnant diet, the blood bank is dropping off your order tonight. I'll leave a check on the table in the foyer."

He rolled his eyes. "Thanks, Mom."

Thank goodness for the new vamp meals-on-wheels program. You'd be amazed how many people would be happy to donate to the cause. Some people thought there was something romantic about the idea. Most just didn't want a town full of thirsty vamps. I couldn't blame them on that count.

I'd seen Shane after his change, when he was still deranged with the bloodlust. The Vamp Council had kept him caged in the basement of their local safe house for almost two weeks before they called me to come get him. At first, the call surprised me. I was still licking my wounds from my cancelled wedding. He'd taken off, or so I'd thought. Their call gave me a sick kind of hope. Maybe he didn't blow me off after all; maybe we could still have our wedding, our life, just like we planned. Seeing him in those chains had been the last straw for me. When you were looking into the blood-red eyes of a vampire, there was nothing romantic about it. He'd grabbed for me, trying to rip my throat out. Part of me wanted to let him; it would have hurt less to have my throat ripped out than my heart.

Something between us broke that day. I'd left him in that cage, unable to make myself believe what had happened. And a few days later, he'd shown up on my door. For a few minutes, it was like it had all been one long, terrible dream.

And then he bit me.

Maybe Mom was right, maybe his soul was damned. Maybe he was just another unfortunate accident. Either way, the person he used to be—the person I loved—was lost to me. Now I just struggled to look at him and not hate him. For what he did, what he'd become, and what I wanted him to be. I pinched my nose with my fingers.

"Headache?" he asked.

"Nah, I just didn't get much sleep last night."

"I know. Oh, and you're welcome for saving your life by the way." He smirked.

"We wouldn't have been stuck in that closet in the first place if your 'super nose' would have smelled Young in the house."

He frowned. "All I could smell was the vamp blood. I thought someone might be hurt."

I waved my hand. "Bygones. Besides, watching you get tranqued with a blowgun was totally worth the price of admission. It was like watching an elephant fall asleep at the zoo. In slow motion."

"An elephant? Surely, you mean a ferocious tiger."

"Or a baboon."

He growled.

I laughed. "You should go change. I have a few calls to make before we leave."

"Are you kicking me out?"

"Darn, and here I thought I was being subtle. Guess I'm no match for your awesome brain power."

"As long as you can admit it."

I made a shooing motion with my hand. "Get out."

"Going. I have a few calls to make myself. Mercy wants to talk to me about the initiation into Conclave."

Mercy was Shane's new girlfriend, of the walking-undead variety. I still didn't get it. She was bottle blonde, her accent was as fake as her expensive fingernails, and she honestly thought Madagascar was something you smoked.

"Are they finally taking you off the leper list?" I asked bitterly.

"I know you don't care, but it's my chance to finally be accepted as what I am. It's not just the money and the status. It's nice to be around other people like me."

"Do you really want to break into that world?"

"Well, I don't really belong here anymore. I'd like to belong somewhere."

"I just don't get what you see in her, Shane, seriously."

"She's like me," he snapped.

Mercy was only a few vamp years older than he was, but she'd been made with the permission of the council and had quickly become their favorite pet. It was her voice in his ear telling him he didn't belong here. He wasn't mine anymore—the rational part of my brain knew that. It was the rest of me that didn't get the memo.

"That's a pretty poor reason to be with someone." I snorted.

"What's a *good* reason to be with someone? Enlighten me, Isabel."

"Well..." I paused, taking a drink of my coffee. "You should be with someone who gets your jokes.

Someone who will hold your hand when you're sick. Someone who doesn't think Calvin Klein started the Boxer Rebellion."

"How about someone who I can kiss without wanting to take a bite of? Someone who doesn't get grossed out when I drink a cup of blood, or who looks at me like they *want* me and not like I'm a burden?"

I was so stunned that I didn't know what to say. Partly because he was right, and as guilty as I felt about it, I didn't know how to make it better either. In some ways, having him around helped. In others, it was like picking at old wounds. Neither of us ever seemed quite able to heal.

Shane held up his hand to stop me before I even opened my mouth.

"I'm sorry. That was uncalled for. I just... it's been so long since I could be with someone and not hold myself back. With Mercy, I can let go and just be myself. Fangs and all."

I nodded. How could I begrudge him that?

"Well, you always have a place here, no matter what Zombie Barbie thinks."

But when he smiled, showing just a little too much fang, I cringed. He noticed and closed his mouth tightly.

"I know," he whispered, walking away. As he turned to leave, he added, "But I think I need my own place. Maybe one of the old plantation houses."

"Or a nice crypt with a view," I called after him.

—— ✥ ——

Reggie had all the evidence boxed up for us when we got to the station. Seeing me walk in, he meandered over and threw a thick arm around my shoulders. The top of my head barely hit his shoulder. Not because he was so tall, but I was just that short. Between my height, my petite frame, and my wavy, dark hair, people were always shocked when I told them my occupation. What I said was private investigator—what they heard was midget bounty hunter.

"How's it going, baby girl?" Reggie asked, leading me to his desk.

That had been his nickname for me for as long as I could remember. He'd been one of my dad's best friends when I was growing up, and he'd been especially fond of me. I could always talk him into having a tea party with me when he came to visit. Let me tell you, there was nothing quite as endearing as a two-hundred-and-seventy pound police officer sitting in a small, pink chair sipping imaginary tea with a tiny napkin tucked into his shirt like a bib.

With a squeeze, he let go of me and shook Shane's hand.

"I've been better, Reggie," I admitted.

He nodded. I was sure he'd heard all about it by now. News traveled fast in a place like Charleston.

Shane sat on the edge of the desk. "So, what can you tell us about the Welch case?"

Reggie ran his hand over his nearly bald head before tossing me a thick manila folder.

"It's all in there. Unfortunately, that's all you get to take with you. Those are copies of the official reports. All the evidence, however, stays here." He shrugged apologetically. "Open case and all."

I understood. Chain of evidence. He couldn't risk us compromising anything just in case it ever had to go to trial. Nodding, I opened the file.

"So, is there somewhere we can take a look at this?" Shane asked.

For being a former history teacher, Shane had adjusted well to the life of a PI. He didn't ask a lot of dumb questions, especially around the police. It made things easier on me not to have to constantly school him on police procedure.

Reggie hefted the white box and dropped it into Shane's arms. "Interrogation Room One is open. It's all ours."

In a strange procession, we walked to the room, followed by dozens of curious stares. I tried to ignore them. It was only natural they'd be curious, even suspicious of Shane, and by association, me. No one was outright rude, and that was all I really asked for.

Flicking on the overhead light, we settled around the wooden table. Reggie took a seat in a corner and propped his feet on the table, leaving Shane and me to rummage through the contents of the box.

I examined the bags. "Are these from the house?"

"The house, the car. Even her locker at the school where she taught," Reggie answered in his thick Southern drawl.

"Her computer?"

He shook his head. "No personal computer. We have her phone, but there were no unusual calls made or received. Baby girl, I know her daddy is upset we aren't actively pursuing the case anymore, but we went over every scrap of her life and came up with a big fat nothing. Looks more and more like she just ran away."

"You really think so?" I looked him flat in the eye.

"Aww hell, I dunno. I don't think she'd leave those kids, that's for sure. But you never really know about people, do ya?"

I agreed. People never failed to surprise, and often disappoint.

I pulled out a bag holding a planner. "Anything in this?"

Reggie nodded as he leaned forward and opened the folder containing the notes. "There's a copy of every page in here. It was just her work schedule, the kids' school stuff, and a couple of nail appointments. No red flags."

"Reggie, you know I'm not trying to step on your toes here. I'm sure you guys did all you could. I told her father as much. But if it'll make him feel better to get another set of eyes on this, then that's the least I can do for him. Whether she just took off or not, he lost his child. Those kids lost their mother. So I'll go over every scrap one more time, just to give them what little peace of mind I can offer."

"I know that, baby girl," Reggie said softly. "I wanna put this mess to bed as much as anyone."

His eyes held mine, full of emotions his words would never betray. We'd both been in the search team when she'd first gone missing. Every day there were fewer and fewer volunteers. At the end, there were just five of us. Then they called off the searches all together. No one ever wanted to admit it, but the honest truth was we knew from day one it wasn't a search-and-rescue mission, it was a recovery mission. We never expected to find her alive.

Reggie had been on the police force for over thirty years. I knew his wife wanted him to retire, and I knew why. Jobs like his, cases like this one, they haunted you. I'd only been doing this for a year, and I could already feel the weariness creeping into my bones. How my father had managed twenty-odd years on the force and another ten as a PI, I would never know.

When I'd first taken over the business, Reggie came to see me. He told me that the only thing keeping him sane was his family, that they tethered him to life. Without that, he said, the darkness would eat away at a man's soul. He told me to find my tether.

I was still looking for one.

Two hours and six pages of notes later, we were finished. As Shane and I repacked the box, Reggie handed me the cardboard lid.

He rubbed his head. "You got everything you need?"

"I think so." I slipped the pages of notes into the folder. "I'll call you if we turn anything up."

I tossed the clear bag holding Lisa Welch's purse into the box with a flick of my wrist. *Useless,* I thought with a huff.

Beside me, Shane stiffened.

I looked up. His face was rigid, nostrils flared, mouth in a half snarl.

"Shane?"

Reggie noticed, too. His hand twitched at his side not far from his gun.

"Shane!" I snapped my fingers this time.

He relaxed, looking down as the tension receded from the air around him.

"What is it?" Reggie asked.

Shane picked up the evidence bag I'd tossed and held it out to Reggie. "Can I open this?"

Reggie tilted his head to the side, his hand still hovering near his gun. "No, but I can. Why?"

"I need to smell it," Shane answered quietly, not looking up.

Reggie looked baffled. "Smell it?"

I stepped in before Shane had to explain. "Shane has a highly developed olfactory sense. A thousand times better than any bloodhound. He might be able to smell something on the purse that could give us a clue about her abductor."

I tried to make myself sound more confident than I felt. Truth was, Shane did have a great nose. Unfortunately, the thing he could smell the best was blood. If that bag had been in, near, or around blood, he'd know it.

With deliberate slowness, Reggie took the bag from Shane's hand. Pulling a knife out of his utility belt, he slid the blade across the red seal, squeezed the bag open a fraction, and held it out to Shane.

"Don't touch it," he warned.

Shane looked up, his brown eyes clear, and nodded. I let out a breath. Whatever he was up to, he was at least in control of himself.

Holding the bag carefully under his face, he drew in a deep breath. Then another. Closing his eyes, he handed the bag back to Reggie, who quickly resealed and initialed the pouch.

"Anything?" Reggie and I asked at the same time.

Shane shook his head. "A hint of perfume and gasoline. This was found in the car?"

"Yep. Wow, that's better than a bloodhound Brooks." Reggie closed the box with a smile. His voice was dry, husky. As much as he liked him, I knew Reggie would have shot Shane in a second if he thought he was going to lose it. I wasn't sure how I felt about that.

"Can we get a look at it?" Shane asked as we left the room.

"You'll have to talk to the husband," Reggie answered. "As soon as the scene was cleared, the car went back to him."

"Great." I sighed.

CHAPTER 4

It was too late for a drop-in visit, so I settled for making a phone call when we got back to the office. Shane sat across from me as I dialed Robert Welch, Lisa's husband. He answered on the first ring, his voice hopeful. I frowned. After all these months, he was still waiting for *the call*. The one that would change his world forever.

"Hello, Mr. Welch. I'm Isabel Stone from Stone Private Investigations. Your father-in-law has hired me to look into your wife's disappearance and..."

That was as far as I got.

"Look here, lady, I don't care who hired you, and I don't want anything to do with it. I've already said everything I'm going to say to the police. Don't call me again."

Click.

I held the phone away from my head and shrugged at Shane, who was tapping a pen on the desk. I knew he'd overheard the brief conversation. Lowering the receiver back into the cradle, I sighed and rested my head on my hands.

"Ok, partner. What did you really smell in that bag?"

With a flick of his wrist, he tossed the pen toward the cup. It landed inside with a thunk. Wiping his hand down his face, he hesitated before he answered. It was a gesture I knew all too well, one that meant I probably wasn't going to like what he had to say.

"I smelled vampire," he finally admitted. "I think."

"You think, super nose? Or are you sure?"

He sat back. "I'm pretty sure."

"Do you know whose scent it was?"

I knew that most vamps had a smell unique to them, and they could often recognize each other by the scent alone. Of course, Shane was a newbie and didn't know many other vamps. At least as far as I was aware.

He shook his head. "I didn't recognize it. But if I could get a stronger whiff, like maybe from the car, then who knows?"

I frowned. "I don't think the husband is going to let us get anywhere near that car."

"So what are our options?"

"I can think of one, but you aren't going to like it."

"Why?" he asked, narrowing his eyes suspiciously.

"Look, if I'm going to call in a favor this big on your hunch, I want to be sure it's not a waste of time. So are you positive you scented vampire?"

"Yes, one hundred percent. Who are you going to call?"

"Ghostbusters," I said sarcastically. Opening the file that held the photocopied info on the car, I picked up the phone. "I'm calling Tyger."

Shane slammed his hand on the cradle. "No, you're not."

Patrick Wallis, aka Tyger, was one of my oldest friends. We'd been inseparable until we turned twelve and his lifestyle drove a wedge between us. By *lifestyle,* I didn't mean a sudden desire to dress in Prada and sing show tunes.

Currently, Tyger was the leader of a local motorcycle gang and had been in and out of jail more times than I could count. When I first took over the office, I was hired to look into a string of burglaries in the upscale side of downtown Charleston. Tyger was arrested for the crimes, but I eventually caught the real thief, a rival gang member trying to get him put away so he could usurp his leadership position. Tyger was grateful, and for a few days, I was really glad I'd been able to help him. That was, until the thief had been beaten almost to death while out on bail. I didn't have any proof that Tyger was behind it, but I believed down to my toes he was. Calling to ask him for a favor was a risk. And from the look on Shane's face, not one he wanted me to take.

"Shane, it might be the only way to get our hands on that car. If you have any better ideas, I'm all ears."

I left it hanging in the air between us. If Shane was really on to something, then this might be our only lead. We could get a hold of the car or we were sunk before we began swimming. I could see from his expression that he was weighing the options.

Finally, he made a dismissive motion with his hand. "Fine. Make the call."

The only number I had for Tyger was the bike shop he owned. They were closed, so I left a message asking him to call me.

Behind me, Shane pulled out the rolling white board and cleaned it off. Together we reconstructed, as best we could, a time line of the day Lisa Welch disappeared.

We worked until the scent of dry-erase markers started giving me a headache and the end result was less than impressive. The police had tracked Lisa's day from eight AM, when she took her kids to school, up to four PM, when she called her neighbor. She said she was "running late" and asked if they could pick the kids up from the bus and keep them until she got home at five.

Lisa Welch was never seen or heard from again.

I stepped back, looking at the time line.

"Okay." I pointed. "She had lunch with her sister Marlene from eleven forty-five 'til about one-fifteen. Marlene told police Lisa was agitated about something, but wouldn't say what and didn't mention anything about her plans for the rest of the day. Lisa paid for lunch, and they went their separate ways. Lisa's car was found abandoned at eleven that night at the Old Town Mall."

"Do we have copies of the financials?"

I rifled through the stacks of papers Reggie had allowed us to copy and tossed Shane the bank and credit card statements.

"The police say there were no unusual charges on either the bank card or her Visa." I continued tapping the dry-erase marker on my chin as Shane leafed through the statements.

"Apparently, she didn't pay for lunch either. At least, not with either of these accounts. Where did they eat?"

I checked Marlene's statement. "The Brand Steakhouse. Maybe she paid cash?"

"Pricey place. When was the last time you paid for a seventy-dollar meal with cash?"

"Good catch," I stated, impressed. "It might be worth checking with the sister."

"Maybe Lisa had a credit card the husband didn't know about. Especially if she were hiding something."

Shane was right. I'd seen that before. It was pretty common with cheating spouses for one to have a secret account. Heck, some had whole secret lives, including houses and cars.

"I'll call Marlene in the morning," I offered.

"No offense, but after the reaction you got from the husband, maybe I should take a stab at this one. The file says she waits tables down at Club Rouge off Peach Street. I could go work my charm on her."

I gritted my teeth. He was right again. Something about him had total strangers ready to spill their life stories to him. Even before becoming a vampire, he'd been charismatic. When you added the otherworldly aura, it was downright unsettling. At least to me. Everyone else found him irresistible.

"Fine," I agreed reluctantly.

Shane flashed a dimpled smile and tossed me the marker he'd been holding.

"Don't wait up," he hollered over his shoulder as

he walked out of the office.

Watching him leave, I hoped I was doing the right thing sicking him on Marlene. The poor girl probably wouldn't know what hit her.

CHAPTER 5

Shane bounced in from Club Rouge just after three AM, looking like the cat that ate the canary. I raised my eyebrow as he talked.

"...Marlene told me that good old Robert had a history of gambling problems. A few years ago, Lisa discovered some of her grandmother's jewelry missing. She suspected Robert hocked it to play the ponies, or at least that's what Lisa told her. Lisa made him start going to Gamblers Anonymous until he had it under control. Also, Lisa did use a credit card to pay for lunch."

"There wasn't anything about this in the police file." That surprised me. They'd dug into Robert Welch with a fine-tooth comb, even after his alibi cleared him as a suspect.

"She said she'd totally forgotten about it until I asked about the credit card, because that day Lisa was wearing one of the missing rings. She noticed it when Lisa handed the card to the waitress."

I was impressed. "Well done, Shane. Anything else?"

He grinned. "She asked me out this weekend. I had to let her down gently. The poor girl was totally into me."

I rolled my eyes. "That's great. Tomorrow, I'm going to see if I can find out where the Gamblers Anonymous meetings were and talk to a few people there. It'd really help if you called your computer guy tonight to see if he could track Lisa's movements from the steakhouse using the traffic cameras in the area. Also, according to the records, she used her cell phone to call and check her home messages at a little after two o'clock. Maybe he can do his tech voodoo and pinpoint where she was when she made the call."

Shane nodded. His one useful connection in the vampire world was Richard Clark. Richard was over a hundred years old and could make a computer stand up and sing Jimmy Buffet songs if he wanted it to. Oh, and he was kind of evil. Like, invented *Wal-Mart* evil. Shane and Richard had both been changed by a vampire named Irena Tarkeroff. It sort of made them brothers.

"Sure. I'll pay him a visit."

Did I mention that Richard was extremely paranoid and reclusive? I'd asked Shane once if I could meet the tech genius, but he'd told me Richard was dangerously unstable around humans. Too many years of feeding off them had left him with little in the way of self-control. And Irena wasn't exactly the maternal type. She tended to turn and run, leaving her newbie vampires to fend for themselves. Lucky for Shane, he'd been found right away. Richard hadn't been so lucky. According to Shane, Richard was changed and abandoned to roam the back alleys of London, feeding off street people. He was finally captured by the local Conclave in 1889 and caged until they could calm him—over fifty years later. Now he was a hermit, content to tinker with computers from the safety of his basement beneath Conclave.

I didn't ask to meet him again.

With a nod of thanks, I clicked off my desk lamp. "I'm going to bed. I'm exhausted."

"Yeah, you should rest. You look like crap." Shane snickered.

Too tired to verbally shoot back, I locked up the office, trudged upstairs to my room, and crawled into bed.

When I woke up the next morning, there was a note from Shane stuck to the already-brewing coffee pot.

Isabel,

I need to talk to you about the initiation next week. Please keep an open mind. Also, I left the street camera footage from Richard on your laptop. You can thank me later.

~Shane

Shaking my head I poured myself a cup of hot coffee and opened the laptop Shane had left on the kitchen counter.

The file was on the desktop labeled 'Shane is

Awesome,' and proved to be a slide show of images from traffic cameras and ATM machines that ended with Lisa's car parked outside The Broken Plow, a downtown antique shop. She was feeding the parking meter. With a silent thanks to Shane and Richard, I closed the screen, took another sip of coffee, and plotted my day.

I started by going over the case files one more time. Before I knew it, noon had come and gone with no word from Tyger. I tracked down the Gamblers Anonymous group's meeting place. For being anonymous, they really didn't fly under the radar well. They had a full-page ad in the Yellow Pages. I scribbled the address on a sticky note.

The group was meeting at the new headquarters for the Church of Redeeming Sacrifice. The CRS, an offshoot of several faiths, was openly opposed to the new vampire legislation some lawmakers were trying to push through. CRS members wanted to go back to the good old days where you could kill a vampire for no other reason than that they were soulless monsters who stood as an affront to God... yada, yada, yada. They weren't the only faith to come out opposed to the vampires, but they were the only one I knew of actively hunting them down.

So much for delegating this chore to Shane, I thought grumpily. In fairness, I might have been in a better mood, but I suspected he was spending his free time with his new girlfriend, and she got under my skin. So naturally, in my opinion, any time they spent together was a waste of it. That and Shane was supposed to be my partner. Leaving me to do the grunt work just sucked.

The meetings were nightly at seven and open to anyone. I loaded up my purse with some of my new goodies and slipped my Glock into my back waistband holster. Pairing my faded denim jeans and white cami with a lightweight jacket just long enough to hide my gun, I was ready. My purse was small, so I could carry either an extra clip or lipstick. When you had to choose between makeup and ammunition, you knew your evening was off to a shaky start. With a quick glance in the mirror, I grabbed my bag and headed out. It was still early, but my first destination wasn't someplace I wanted to visit in the dark.

Maybe it was a good thing Shane wasn't with me after all.

Walking into Tyger's motorcycle shop, I was glad I'd chosen the extra clip. One downside to having friends in places like this was that you weren't always sure they were, in fact, your friends. Would the fact that once upon a time we'd dug mud caves together keep him from telling me to kiss his ass? I was hoping so. That and the fact that I occasionally bailed him out of jail.

Trying to look more confident that I felt, I walked up to the counter, recognizing the man behind it. It was Brian 'Tiny' Rodriguez. He was about 6'9" and 360 lbs. of *imposing*. He'd earned the nickname *Tiny* the way a bald man became *Harry* or my uncle who'd lost three fingers in a sheet-metal accident had become *Lefty*.

Tiny's head was shaved so you got a full view of the snake tattoo that ran up his neck, around his ear, and up to the crown of his skull. Funny, it looked smaller in his mug shot.

"Hey. I'm looking for Tyger."

"You found him," a voice answered from the back room.

I leaned over and saw him sitting at a workbench, packing bearings. With one finger, he motioned for me to come in. I did, closing the door behind me.

Tyger wasn't quite as impressive as Tiny, but he was close. A comfortable six-plus feet tall, he wore black jeans and a white wife beater smudged with grease and oil. He was ripped like a professional bodybuilder, the muscle so defined it was almost over the top. His freshly shaved scalp was decorated with a tribal tattoo that began somewhere on his back and ran up to his crown where it came to a spear point. He had enough silver hoops in his face to make a TSA agent cry, the largest being a bull ring through his septum. All that aside, when he smiled at me, we were nine again, and he was about to ask to share my pudding cup.

"Isabel, it's been a while. How've you been?"

I sat down on the stool across from him. "Good. You? Keeping out of trouble, I hope."

He snickered, not looking up from the metal in his hands, but he didn't answer.

"I'm here because I need a favor," I began hesitantly.

He set the bearing down, grabbed a blue rag, and wiped off his fingers. "What would a solid citizen like you need from a guy like me?"

I pulled the ring across the bench, scooped a handful of grease, and finished packing the bearings as Tyger pulled the next piece off the old motorcycle.

"I need you to get a hold of a car for me."

He laughed. "You need me to boost a car for you. Are you kidding? You wearing a wire under there?" A mischievous smile played at his mouth as he pointed a dirty finger toward my blouse.

I shook my head and wiped off my hands. "I'm on a case. There might be evidence in that car that I need. I just want to borrow it for a few hours."

"Hypothetically, I might be able to help you with your case. But it'll cost you."

I sighed. "How much?"

"Please, girl. I don't want your money."

"Then what do you want?"

"I need a new security system here in the shop. See, last month the books came up short by a couple of hundred bucks. I need to know who's cookin' the numbers, you feel me?"

I nodded. "I assume you keep everything on your computer?"

"Of course."

"All right, show me." I really didn't want to test my new keystroke recorder just yet, but I supposed it was a fair trade, much better than what I'd thought he was going to ask for. It was a good thing I'd packed my gadgets.

I installed the device and turned it on.

"There," I said closing the computer back up. "We should have some answers soon. Now, for your part of the deal."

I took out one of my business cards, wrote Robert Welch's address and the plate number on it, and handed it to him.

"It was good to see you, Patrick."

He cringed. "Don't let anybody hear you call me that. And Isabel, take care of yourself."

I nodded. "I will."

The office was quiet when I got back. I didn't intend to stay too long, but I needed to change out of my tall leather boots into less conspicuous-looking footwear before the GA meeting. But whenever I stopped at the house, I had to check the machine. There was message from my mother wanting me to come over for dinner. Apparently, Phoebe had a new boyfriend Mom wanted me to discreetly investigate. Mom thought he was "shifty."

I sighed and jotted down his information.

The next message was a man's voice crackling through the machine.

"Isabel. I just thought you should know I'm out on bail. We should get together, grab a drink. Maybe I'll swing by your place some time." Then the caller just laughed and hung up.

A shiver shot up my back. I recognized the laugh. I'd heard it through a closet door just before a house was set on fire with Shane and me inside. It was Billy Young. I was on the phone with Reggie in a matter of seconds.

He answered his cell with, "What's up, baby girl?"

"Reggie, were you gonna mention that the arsonist I helped catch was out on bail?"

I could hear him sit up in his squeaky desk chair. "I didn't know he was."

"Well, he called my place today. Said he'd stop by some time."

Reggie cussed. "You need me to get a car out

there, keep an eye on things?"

I thought about it. Suddenly, the gun in the small of my back felt really good.

"Naw. I'll let Shane know, but I've got pretty good security here. Just do me a favor and find the SOB, okay? And when you do, haul him in for harassment. I'll press charges if I need to."

"Okay, sugar. You be careful now, a'right?"

"Always am." I hung up the phone.

Shane walked in the front door a minute later with Mercy in tow. I could hear her annoying voice well before her face came into the office.

Mercy had been young when she turned, only nineteen according to Shane, and she still acted like a permanent teenager. In a leaves-nothing-to-the-imagination red sundress and wearing dozens of bangle bracelets, she flowed into the room as if she were a movie star walking the red carpet. My hand twitched at my back, wanting desperately to shoot a few holes in her pretty face.

"Isabel, so nice to see you again," she said with a Southern drawl so strong that she could pass for Scarlett O'Hara in a remake of *Gone with the Wind*.

I ignored Mercy. "Shane, Young made bail somehow. Slippery little weasel. Keep an eye out in case he comes snooping around here, all right?"

That was when I noticed he was holding her hand. My trigger finger twitched again.

"I will. But if you've got a second, we need to talk to you about the initiation next week." He led Mercy to a chair in the sitting room.

"Uh-huh," I managed, sitting as far away from them as the small room would allow.

"You see," Mercy began, the words rolling out of her mouth like molasses, "the Council has decided to welcome our Shane into vampire society. They plan to hold his initiation during the annual vampire ball. It's tradition that his sire and a member of his human family attend. As his sire is no longer available..."

That was a nice way to put it, I thought. *'No longer available.'*

"...I will be acting in her stead. We were hoping, since Shane's human family isn't able to attend, that you might act as his family for the evening."

I looked from her to Shane. Was this some sort of joke? The expression on his face told me it wasn't. The look was half embarrassed, half hopeful, and all Shane. I wanted to refuse him, I really did. But something in the pit of my stomach wouldn't let me, couldn't bear to disappoint him or let him down. Even after all we'd been through.

"I'm really going to regret this," was my answer.

Mercy clapped merrily and Shane smiled, nodding with a subtle bow of his head that I returned.

"It'll be perfect. We'll get you something suitable to wear, of course," Mercy rambled on until my eyes glazed over.

I decided to get the hell out of there before Shane could manipulate me any further with his puppy-dog eyes. With a less-than-heartfelt goodbye, I was out the door in a flash. I'd rather have taken on a pack of rabid honey badgers than spend another second making small talk with Mercy.

The Gamblers Anonymous meetings were held in the meeting room at the Church of Redeeming Sacrifice. The CRS had opened its doors shortly after the vamps had their little coming out about two years before. The most aggressively outspoken faction when it came to the "Demonic aberrations," the CRS's official opinion held that vampires should be staked on sight. And there were a whole lot of people that agreed with them. I mean, would you want a vampire teaching your kids? Operating on you? Hell, driving your taxi at two AM? I wasn't saying they were right, only that I sort of understood why people might be afraid.

I'd seen a raging vampire up close and personal. Heck, I lived with one. The difference was, most of the time it was just the same old Shane I'd gotten to know in college. The guy I'd fallen in love with. Most of the time, I still saw that guy in his eyes.

Just walking through the chapel's Gothic double doors gave me the creeps. Or maybe it was the fresco on the ceiling that depicted a dozen winged angels holding down a vampire and tearing off its head that made my stomach turn. I walked the halls until I found the only occupied room in the building. The meeting room was small, with only ten chairs squeezed into a semi-circle. The smell of stale donuts and strong coffee hung in the air. Two chairs sat empty.

As soon as I entered the doorway, the intimate group all turned to gawk at the new face. Fighting back a blush, I gave an awkward wave and slid into an empty seat next to a woman in her late forties wearing a red, midriff-bearing tank top, with matching shorts and cowboy boots.

"Go on, no one is here to judge you." The man sitting in the middle of the semi-circle gave the man next to him an encouraging pat on the shoulder.

I recognized the supporter from the news. It was Charles Marlowe, leader of the CRS and their self-proclaimed preacher. Apparently, he also served as judge, jury, and executioner of the vampire scourge. Just last week, he'd been calling people to arms against the federal government's decision to grant vampires temporary legal status until the legislature could devise a more permanent solution. Yes, the man sitting across from me in his blue polo shirt and Dockers, was, down to the tips of his shiny loafers, a bigot.

"Well, when Mary found out I'd taken out the second mortgage on the house, she packed up the kids and moved to her mother's place in Memphis," a scruffy-looking man continued what he'd been saying before I'd entered.

A murmur of sympathy carried though the room.

"Well, can you blame her, Paul?" Charles asked.

Now crying, Paul shook his head, face obscured by withered hands.

In unison, the group chimed in, "We will overcome. We will not be controlled by our vices. Together, we are strong. United, we can make ourselves better."

With a round of applause, the meeting was over. I breathed a sigh of relief at having gotten in at the end of the session so I didn't have to make up some lame excuse for crashing. Hanging back, I watched as the people grabbed a quick snack and a cup of coffee before filing out. One woman, the only other female in the group besides Tank Top Lady and me, held out an overly bejeweled hand. Even her perfectly manicured fingernails had tiny white crystals embedded in the pink polish.

"Hey. I'm Trudi. Trudi Polk. I run the dry cleaners down on Pear Street. Are you a new member?"

I smiled my best sweet smile and shook her hand. "Well, I'm just checking things out. I don't actually have a gambling problem."

She winked. "Neither do I, sugar. I just come for the coffee and to see Pastor Marlowe, of course. Poor thing. Lost his wife two summers ago and his daughter, Melanie, sick with the Cystic Fibrosis. He needs a good woman to help him along, don't you think?" she asked as she looked past me, her face filling with adoration as she caught the pastor's eye.

Pastor Marlowe's returning glance her direction was a smile that thinly veiled a grimace.

For a member of an 'anonymous' association, Trudi sure was a talker. I smiled conspiratorially. People like Trudi made my job much easier.

"So, how long have you been coming to these meetings?" I asked casually as I helped myself to a Styrofoam cup of a coffee-like substance.

She folded her arms across her chest, making the most of her minimal cleavage while she tossed her bottle-blonde hair over her shoulder. "Let's see... about a year now."

"Ah. My friend suggested I come. Maybe you know him, Robert Welch?"

The name got her attention.

"No, I never met him, personal-like, but I read all about that poor man's misfortune. If you ask me, that no-good wife of his done took off and left him with those precious little children. Jessica, the lady who does my nails, told me she knew the missing lady and that she was in the salon real regular. Always tanning and waxing and getting her nails done." She wagged her eyebrows suggestively. "Only one reason a married woman goes to all that trouble."

"You think she was cheating?" I asked carefully.

She touched her chest with her fingertips. "Well, I'm not one to gossip. That's just my opinion. Got no proof, mind you. I suppose it's between her and the Good Lord, but if you ask me, that woman's gonna rot in H-E-double-toothpicks for what she did."

I would have continued to tap the font of information in snakeskin pumps that was Trudi Polk, but we were interrupted.

"Ladies. Trudi, good to see you as always."

She beamed as her name slipped past Marlowe's lips. He held his hand out to me. "However, I don't believe we've met."

I took his hand. "I'm Isabel. I was actually hoping to speak to you alone for a minute, Pastor."

Beside me, Trudi frowned. She hadn't thought of me as competition until that second. It was amazing to me how quickly some girls were willing to cat fight over men that didn't even belong to them.

"Certainly," he said, relief spreading across his face, probably at the excuse to escape Trudi's amorous intentions. With a wave of his hand, he ushered me from the room and up the hallway to a door on the right marked PRIVATE. Behind us, one of the men from the group sprinted forward.

"I got everything put away, and the room is ready for nursery school Sunday. Is there anything else, Pastor?"

"No, David. But thank you. This is Miss Isabel..." He paused, probably remembering that I hadn't told him my last name.

I stuck out my hand, and David took it. His hands were harsh, dry, and calloused—a stark contradiction to his neat suit-and-tie ensemble. More blue collar than blue tie, but he was obviously trying to play the part.

"Stone. Isabel Stone. It's nice to meet you."

"David Pierce." He nodded curtly after holding my eyes for a second longer than was really necessary.

He turned back to Marlowe. "All right, Pastor. I'm heading home. Call me if you need anything."

Marlowe nodded before turning to unlock his office door, and David made his way down the hall toward the exit. That precaution was smart but inconvenient if I needed to break in later. Hopefully, it wouldn't come to that, but the way my week was going, who knew?

"David is my assistant," Marlowe explained as he waved me into the office. "A devout man and a personal friend. I don't know what I'd do without him most days."

Taking a seat across from his desk, I noticed a picture of two women I presumed to be his wife and daughter on one side and a stack of what looked like medical files on the other.

"What can I do for you today, Miss Stone?" he asked, leaning back in his chair, voice not quite as friendly as it had been.

"I wanted to ask you some questions about your parishioners, the Welch family."

He frowned, tapping his fingers on the edge of his desk.

"Ah, so you're looking into the disappearance. You are the proprietor of Stone Private Investigations, are you not? I thought your name sounded familiar."

I nodded. "I am. We've been hired by Lisa's father, Mr. Curtis."

"It's unfortunate he felt it necessary to go to such lengths. Lisa's disappearance has been extremely hard on him, on them all. I didn't know Lisa; she wasn't a regular parishioner here. Robert has been coming for some time, though."

"I understand he used to have quite a gambling problem."

As I expected, he shot me down.

"Isabel, surely you understand that I can't discuss the private lives of our followers. I will say only that Robert is a good man and a good father. I don't believe for a moment he could ever hurt his wife, or anyone for that matter. He has what we call common *human* decency."

I was totally prepared to let it go. In fact, I stood up to leave, a thank-you forming on my lips. Marlowe stood up as well, leaning across the desk.

"Isabel, I know about your situation. If you ever need help, someone to assist you in ridding yourself of the creature that you work with, please come to us. We do the Lord's work here, no matter how dangerous. You don't have to be afraid anymore."

I laughed. I didn't mean to. He was being so earnest, treating me like a battered wife scared to leave her abusive spouse, but I snickered anyway. In hindsight, not the best reaction.

When I was finally able to compose myself, I responded, leaning over the desk until our noses were almost touching. "Thanks for the offer, Pastor. But Shane is my partner, my *friend*, and he's not going anywhere. He has more common decency in his little finger than most of the humans I know."

I spun on my heel and made it to his office door before he called after me.

"You can't trust their kind. They are soulless, evil. If you choose to stand with them, you will eventually get hurt."

I glared at him. "That's funny. Just a couple of days ago, a plain, old human tried to burn me alive, and that soulless, evil vampire saved me. Maybe he didn't get the memo about all the *human* decency."

With that, I walked out, slamming his door behind me. I was halfway down the hall when a voice called out to me.

"Miss Stone?" It was David Pierce.

I took a deep breath, trying to calm myself before I turned. "Yes?"

He caught up to me. David was in brown slacks and an off-white, button-up shirt with a crimson tie. He reminded me of a salesman at Sears. "I couldn't help overhearing, and I just want to apologize. Pastor Marlowe is a good man, but he can be a bit *overzealous.*"

I held back my usual snarky comeback. The

wheels in my brain were turning at full steam. Marlowe's assistant might be a handy asset. I smiled.

"I understand. I didn't mean to lose my temper. He just struck a nerve."

"About your partner, the vampire?"

I shrugged. Biting my bottom lip, I decided quickly that if I was going to get any info, a change of approach might be in order. I opted for the heartbroken damsel routine.

"We were engaged, you know, back when he was still human. Now things are so... complicated."

"Are you afraid he might hurt you?"

I exhaled, trying to decide what answer would get him on my side and not get Shane chased down with a flamethrower.

"No, he's harmless. But the others, well, you never know. I mean, they *look* so human. Sometimes, you forget what they're capable of."

He nodded, looking straight ahead as we walked toward the parking lot.

"Well," he pushed the door open and held it for me, "just remember that the CRS is always here for you if you need us. We really do care. We're family here."

I smiled and thanked him before walking alone to my car. He must have turned around and gone back inside because when I reached my car door, he was gone.

Shane and Mercy were gone when I got home, not a huge surprise. Mercy wasn't stupid. Well, okay, she really was. She still must have felt my not exactly subtle I-want-to-rip-your-face-off vibes.

Wide awake, with my body still humming with anger, I settled in to watch a movie. Afterwards, I did the dishes and then dusted. Rage cleaning, my mom called it. For me, it was more of a way to clear my head. When I finally crawled to bed at three AM, they still weren't back. Not that I was waiting for them. It wasn't enough that Shane had guilted me into going to the stupid vampire cotillion, but to add insult to injury, Mercy insisted I wear a traditional gown that would be provided for me by the Council. I was betting on something frilly and pink. *Spiffy*.

I fell asleep wondering what pink taffeta looked like on fire.

I was still drooling on my pillow when the phone rang downstairs. My clock blinked 10:13 AM in bright red numbers. With a groan, I pulled my pillow over my head and let the machine answer. But as soon as I heard the voice, I sprang out of bed. Still in boxer shorts and sleep tee, tangled in my sheets, I fell to the floor with a thud and a grunt. I scrambled down the stairs to the office, grabbed the phone off the hook, and answered, breathless.

"Hello?"

Dial tone. I'd been a heartbeat too late and the machine had caught it.

Hitting the playback button, I dropped into my desk chair to listen.

"Isabel, it's Tyger. I don't know if you've heard, but somebody boosted a car last night. Left it over in the parking lot behind Bojangles on 3rd St. What's this town coming to?" He laughed. "Hope you find what you're looking for today."

Click. The grin that spread across my face made me feel a bit like the Grinch.

"And my heart grew three sizes that day," I muttered to no one.

I glanced up the stairs to Shane's door. It was closed, so I knew immediately he was home. He only closed his door when he was inside.

After a cup of coffee and a quick shower, I changed into something subtle—a pair of dark jean shorts with a faded gray T-shirt and a pair of cowboy boots. I wanted to be inconspicuous, but I didn't want to look like a cat burglar either. With my second cup of coffee in hand, I tapped on Shane's door. No answer. He was probably still dead to the world, pun intended.

I tapped again, harder this time. "Shane?"

Still nothing.

Taking a deep breath, I turned the knob and cracked the door. I realized with a gasp that Shane wasn't alone and slammed the door quickly. Surely, that had been an elbow, knee, or something peeking out of the messy bed covers.

I gagged a little. Did they make soap for the eyeballs?

Slipping back to my room, I reached around on the top shelf of my closet until my hand curled over the object I'd been looking for. It was a souvenir from a hockey game my dad had taken me to when I was fourteen, and now it was part of my private arsenal. I tossed it up in the air and caught it, hoping there was still a little juice left from the last time I'd used it. Returning to Shane's door, I cracked it, slipped my arm in the gap, and hit the button.

The air horn wailed, echoing throughout the entire house, quickly followed by the loud thud of two bodies hitting the floor. I pushed the button once more for good measure.

"Hey, Count Suckula," I hollered, "we've got the car. You still wanna go check it out or what?"

Mercy growled behind the door, a feral, wild sound like a mountain lion. Shane whispered something that quieted her, and then called to me, "I'll be down in a few minutes."

"You have five, and then I'm going without you."

I was sitting downstairs in my dad's favorite burnt-orange recliner. It was horrifically ugly, but it smelled of Old Spice and analgesic balm—like my father—so it had a permanent place in my house. I was nestled comfortably when Mercy practically flew downstairs to do her walk of shame. Seeing me, she snarled. I waved, blowing her a kiss. Her pretty face twisted, and she lunged into my living room, eyes flashing red.

I held up the squirt gun in my hand, waving it. "Ah, ah, ah," I tisked. "Wouldn't want things to get messy."

She stopped, looking confused for a minute, and then laughed. "What, are you going to soak me to death?"

Now it was my turn to laugh. "I guess that depends on the *type* of water inside, doesn't it?"

For a second, she looked confused again—probably the natural resting state of her face, but then realization dawned on her. "Holy water wouldn't kill me," she retorted, but her tone wasn't entirely confident.

She was right—pouring it on her skin wouldn't kill her. But it would burn like acid and it would be extremely painful and slow to heal.

"True, but it would mess up that pretty face of yours, wouldn't it, Mercy?" I drew out her name until it sounded like a curse. "Do you think Shane would still like you if half your face was melted off?"

Ok, that was bitchy. But I didn't really care at the moment. This was my house, and she was an unwelcome visitor.

She snorted but took a step back, pointing at me. "You shouldn't wound anything you can't kill."

I smiled. "Don't worry. I won't."

Stuffing a wide-brimmed hat on her head, she donned a pair of sunglasses so big that they swallowed half her face.

"See you next week, sugar," she called over her shoulder to Shane, back to her saccharine-sweet Scarlett voice as she slammed my front door behind her.

As soon as she was gone, Shane came trotting down the stairs, hair still wet from the shower. I laughed before he saw me. He, too, was wearing dark jeans and a gray shirt. We were matchy.

He glared as he turned to the kitchen, pulled open the fridge, and grabbed a blood bag. Tearing open the corner with his teeth, he poured it into a coffee mug and joined me in the sitting room.

"What the hell was all that about?" he demanded before taking a long drink.

I smiled and shrugged, the water pistol still in my hand. Seeing it, he frowned.

"What did you say to Mercy?"

I gave him my best wide-eyed innocent look, "I have no idea what you mean."

He nodded to the gun. "Holy water? Was that really necessary?"

I shrugged again and squirted him in the arm.

He jumped, nearly spilling his cup'o blood.

I snickered and tossed the gun onto the coffee table. "It's just tap water. And watch the carpet—that stuff stains."

"And the air horn? That was just uncalled for," he chastised me, wiping his arm off with his free hand.

It was mean, I knew. Vampire senses were much stronger than humans. Everything was enhanced, making lights brighter, sounds louder, and scents stronger. It was why most people believed that vampires couldn't walk around in the daylight. They could. Direct sunlight just really hurt their eyes. Shane had told me it got worse as a vampire got older. The really ancient ones didn't go out during the day at all. Besides being super paranoid that they might burst into flames from a paper cut, the heat, smells, and light easily overwhelmed their systems.

What could I say? That I was feeling jealous that my ex-fiancé was shacking up in *my* house with his trampy new girlfriend? Yeah, like I'd admit to that. When hell froze over.

I took a sip of my coffee. "I tried to knock."

"Well, you missed," he said flatly.

CHAPTER 6

The car was right where Tyger said it would be. Of course, the hubcaps were missing. I shook my head, not surprised.

The great thing about Shane was that most of the time, we didn't even have to speak. A look, a gesture, and we could read each other like books. Of course, sometimes that came back to bite me. Like right then.

He must have seen me shake my head because he put a hand on my shoulder. "That's what you get when you work with criminals."

I wanted to say something, to defend my childhood friend. But what could I say, really? Shane was right. So I did what I always did when Shane was right and I was... less right. I flipped him off.

Lisa Welch drove a sickeningly cute VW Beetle in bright yellow. The plates read *Abug8me*. Shane and I donned our blue latex gloves and got to work. The doors were unlocked so we just slipped inside. He closed his eyes and inhaled deeply while I riffled through the contents of the glove box. Nothing but the registration, an insurance card, a gum wrapper, and a small bottle of sunblock.

Shane shook his head. He wasn't getting anything.

"Let's try the trunk," I offered, popping the latch.

We got out and circled around front.

Shane leaned forward, pulled the hatch up, and inhaled. His eyes flew open behind his dark shades. "This is the smell from the purse. Perfume. Gasoline. And definitely vampire."

He took another long sniff.

"There was a vampire in the trunk?"

He shook his head. "The scent isn't so much inside the trunk as peripheral. On the edges. Like he—or maybe she, I guess—was putting something in the trunk. It's very subtle."

"Would you recognize the scent if you smelled it again?" I shut the trunk and turned to look at him.

"Oh yes. It's pretty distinctive."

I didn't ask what he meant by that as I locked the car. We took off our gloves, tossing them in my backseat as we headed to our next stop.

Shane didn't really need to go to the antique store with me, but I'd decided to make him suffer a little. Sure, I could have taken him back to the office, but I wasn't feeling particularly generous towards *His Paleness*, so I made him tag along.

The *Broken Plow* was nestled between a quilting supply shop and the post office, only a few blocks from my mother's bakery. I considered stopping over there for lunch after we scoped the antique store out, then briefly wondered if I was *that* ticked off at Shane. I mean, threatening him with holy water was funny—subjecting him to my mother was just mean.

The bell above the door jingled pleasantly, announcing our entrance. The store was set up sort of like a library with rows of shelves on either side of a central walkway. Only instead of books, the shelves held various knickknacks and baubles. Stacks of old magazines covered in dust, ornate plates, teacups, vinyl record albums, toys, jewelry, radios—if you could name it, it was probably on a shelf.

Shane went rigid beside me. His shoulders pulled back, his jaw tightened, and the muscles in his neck and arms tensed. I could feel it radiating off him in waves of cold, like I'd just opened the refrigerator door. I swore the temperature in the room dropped ten degrees. Putting a hand on his shoulder, I gave him a questioning look.

Before I could say anything, a saleslady appeared from nowhere.

"Can I help y'all find something?" She smiled.

I turned to look at her. She was tall for a woman, dressed in a flowing purple skirt and matching peasant top. Her pale blonde hair was in a loose bun at the top of her head. Several wild tendrils hung down.

Before I could say anything, Shane rushed past me in a blur of vampire speed. When I blinked, he had the woman pinned against the back wall of the store, his fingers white around her tan throat.

"Where?" Shane demanded.

I tried to reach for him, but he slapped me away

with his free hand while the woman struggled to wrench his other hand off her throat.

"Where's what? Shane, she can't breathe!" I shouted.

"Where?" Shane repeated.

It wasn't a question. I watched as the woman's panicked eyes flashed to cat yellow.

He wasn't asking where. He was identifying the woman as a *were*.

I'd never seen a *were* in person before. While the vamps had made themselves public, the *weres* had remained safely in the darkness. My father had a whole file on the local *were* community that I'd stumbled upon when I took over the office.

A small pack roamed in Charleston, only five or six members. Besides things like breaking down the pack structure and notes on their strengths and weaknesses, my father's file had only one other note in it. A warning that *weres* and vamps were natural enemies. Two apex predators sharing the same territory was a dangerous thing. Seeing Shane's reaction to her, I realized my dad was right.

"Shane... Shane!"

He blinked twice, seeming to come back to himself at the sound of my voice. She slid down the wall as he released her. In a blink, she was behind us, crouched low with her hands extended, human fingers curled like claws.

I stepped between them. "Enough. What is going on?"

Shane sniffed the air. "I smell vampire and *were*. That way." He pointed to a door in the back marked 'Employees Only'.

The woman stood upright, dusting herself off. "You must be the new blood. This area is restricted by order of the Council."

I knew she meant the Vampire Council, the governing body of the Undead. Shane stopped mid-step. I didn't have to read his mind to know what he was thinking. If he defied the Council's orders, the repercussions would be severe. As of now, he stood alone, rogue, but he was hoping to change that. Getting in trouble would put his status change in serious jeopardy.

Luckily, I didn't have that issue. Pushing past him, I opened the door. Beyond it was a staircase leading down to a lower floor. I flicked on the overhead florescent light, took hold of the rusty, steel rail, and headed down. The footsteps behind me were Shane's. Behind him, the *were* woman followed, sounding more irritated than frightened as she told us again that the area was off limits. But she didn't move to stop us. I wondered if she could—take on a vampire, I mean. Me, she could have carved up like a Thanksgiving turkey, even in her human form.

The staircase led down into the underbelly of the building. Brick walls stretched into a room that held a rusty water heater, furnace, and ceiling-to-floor file cabinets. Behind the bottom of the stairs was another closed door. I put my hand on the knob, but Shane grabbed my arm, preventing me from pushing it open. He mouthed the word "vampire" and pulled me behind him. Before he could open the door himself, it swung open, and Xavier Ambrose stepped out.

Xavier was the head of the vampire food chain in South Carolina. His official title was Chancellor to the Council, but his job description was more like that of a feudal lord. He ruled over the Conclave here and all the little vampires in it.

Xavier's was the voice on the phone that had called me to Shane's side after his change. Xavier was the one who had sat me down and explained what had happened to Shane and his sire Irena. And Xavier was the one who had made me choose. I could either assume responsibility for Shane or they'd put him down like a rabid animal. That was the penalty for an unauthorized change.

Looking like he'd just stepped out of some glossy men's magazine, Xavier wore confidence like he wore his casual slacks and button-down blue shirt. He was much less formal than the first time I'd met him. His black hair was hanging limp, hints of waves falling on the pale skin of his face. He wore no tie and his sleeves were rolled to his elbows, but even so, he was completely drool worthy.

It was a common misconception that all vamps were young and attractive, but it was one that worked in their favor, so they used it. Being so good looking, Xavier quickly became the vampire poster boy. It was his handsome face on TV pleading for equality, his earnest, green eyes swearing vampires meant humans no harm.

Yeah, right.

"Xavier," I said, unable to keep the surprise out of my voice.

I knew for a fact that he and the rest of his advisers had offices in the Bank of Charleston building. I also knew it had a basement vault, since Shane had been kept there after his change. So what was he doing in the basement of a *were*-run antique store?

Xavier didn't look at me, choosing to glare at Shane instead.

"You should not be here," he stated flatly.

His tone was cool, professional. A stark contrast from the first time we met, the day he told me what happened to Shane. After the attack, he'd been taken by the Conclave. I thought he'd just run off on me. Somehow, the truth was both better and worse. Still, when he brought me the news, I cried. I cried like a little girl—like I hadn't cried in years. And he'd wrapped his arms around me, holding me until the tears ran dry. It probably wasn't Conclave policy, but it was more kindness than he should have offered a nobody human.

I owed him for that.

Shane bowed stiffly, still keeping one hand on my arm. "I apologize. We will be on our way."

"I told them it was forbidden," the super-helpful *were* woman piped up.

"Thank you, Catherine. That will be all." Xavier dismissed her, turning to a file cabinet and pulling it open.

Shane and I turned to follow Catherine, but Xavier's voice stopped us. So much for sneaking out.

"Why have you come?"

I assumed he was talking to Shane, so I remained quiet.

"We're investigating a disappearance. The woman was last seen in this area. When we came

in to ask if she'd been seen here, I smelled *were...*"
Shane paused. "I wasn't sure what to think. The *were* claimed to be under orders from the Council, but I was unaware we had ties to the *were* clans."

Xavier was fingering through the files. "Yes. Well, fledgling, there is much about the Council you are unaware of. That fact is not likely to change soon. I understand since you are still new, it would be your first instinct not to trust the *were*. However, *you* must understand that your actions do not reflect well on you."

I stepped forward, swallowing a dry lump in my throat. "This was my fault. Shane wasn't going to come down, but he followed me."

Xavier raised one dark eyebrow. "Is this true?"

Shane nodded. "I was afraid she might get into trouble."

Xavier mumbled something I couldn't hear. Shane snickered.

"What disappearance are you investigating?" With a fluid motion, Xavier tugged a manila folder out of the drawer, flicked it open, examined it for a split second, and then returned it to its place with a frustrated sigh. He moved on to the next drawer, flipping through the folder tabs with lightning speed.

It was difficult to pry my eyes off him. Even from the back, Xavier possessed an almost magnetic charisma, not to mention an ass that just begged to be leered at.

Shane glanced at me, snapping me from my half-formed daydream. I shrugged, forcing myself to look away.

While Shane filled Xavier in on our most recent case, I took the opportunity to pace around the room. Most of the walls were lined with large, metal filing cabinets. In the back, a few crates were stacked up. I poked at the straw sticking out between the wooden slats and discovered the crates contained wine bottles. There were no windows. The only lights hung overhead in long, narrow tubes that produced a soft buzzing sound. Walking past the door, I craned my neck to get a peek inside. It was the size of a small closet with a simple wooden desk and black leather chair. On the desk sat a green lamp, an old rotary dial phone, and some sort of ledger lying open with a pen in the fold. I bit my lip, wishing I could get a peek at that book. There was no way the vamps weren't involved in this somehow. Thankfully, Shane managed to leave the part about finding the vampire scent out of the conversation.

After making my way around the room once, I returned to stand beside Shane. Xavier grabbed another folder—apparently, the one he'd been looking for—tucked it under his arm, and slid the drawer closed.

"And you believe we had something to do with this woman going missing?" Xavier asked, this time looking at me.

I took a breath. "This is the last place we tracked her to. It stands to reason that something of a paranormal nature happened. Soccer moms don't just vanish without a trace." *Unless vampires are involved*, I added silently.

"Her name was Lisa Welch, you say?" He turned back to the file cabinets.

"Yes."

Xavier opened a drawer and retrieved another file before slamming it closed and motioning with both hands for us to go upstairs. He followed, turning off the lights as we reached the top step.

Catherine sat on a stool behind the register, reading a soap opera magazine. Xavier waved to her.

"Thank you, Catherine."

She saluted sarcastically and went back to reading.

When we reached the front door, Xavier pressed the second file into my hands. Our fingers touched for only a moment, but the connection was electric, giving us both pause, if only for a heartbeat.

"This may be of some help. I want to assure you, none of my people would have done this thing." His expression was serious—if reserved. He turned to Shane. "Shane, I look forward to your introduction next week. Until then."

He nodded curtly, and then he crossed the street to a sleek, black limo waiting at the curb. As soon as it sped off, I opened the folder.

"What does it say?" Shane asked.

I shook my head, unable to process what I saw. "You aren't going to believe this."

CHAPTER 7

"Lisa Welch was a hooker? I'm just not sure I can wrap my head around that."

Shane propped his feet on the coffee table as I brought out a hot cup of coffee for me and a warm cup of blood for him.

Taking his with one hand, he grumbled, "A paper cup?"

I'd picked up some disposable travel cups at the store, the kind with lids. That way, I at least wouldn't have to watch him drink it. Plus, blood stained white coffee mugs. I'd thrown away four of my favorites before I laid down the law about cup segregation. Unfortunately, I'd discovered that segregation wasn't enough.

"Yeah, you get blood moustaches when you drink out of the big mugs. If you'd prefer, I could pick up a box of bendy straws."

He snorted and took a sip. "No thanks. This is fine."

I took the file back from his lap. According to what we'd read, Lisa Welch was an escort, although what that meant in the vampire world, neither Shane nor I knew. The file also indicated that her husband was in serious debt to a bookie associated with the Conclave, but there were no details on that.

My father had suspected for a long time that the Vampire Council had their fingers in a bit of everything from law enforcement all the way to the highest branches of government. They ran their organization like the Mafia.

The head of the Council was Sekhmet, the oldest known vampire in existence. She and her two advisors, Nichols Von Wielder and Elizabeth Lathery, ruled from a secret location somewhere in North America. While Sekhmet appeared occasionally, she seemed content to allow the regional Chancellors to do the heavy lifting.

Xavier was responsible for the Conclaves in both the Carolinas and Georgia. He also had two advisers, Ahnarra Collins and Gerard Van Swieten. Ahnarra, I'd met. Gerard was more of a mystery.

"Lisa becoming a hooker makes a twisted kind of sense," I stated. "The husband gets in over his head. She goes to the bookie, looking to cut a deal to pay them back. Do you think he knew?"

Shane shrugged. "Nobody else knew. She might have been able to keep it quiet."

I sat back, lacing my fingers together behind my head. "Maybe. They gave her a credit card to use for expenses, but it wasn't found with her belongings. So where is it?"

"I see what you're saying. She either took it and ran off—"

"Which would have earned her a one-way ticket

to a shallow grave for bailing on the Conclave—"

"Or whoever killed her took it back. Assuming, of course, that she's dead."

I nodded. "My gut tells me she's dead. The question is—why?"

Shane and I were still pouring over the new information when a sharp knock came at the front door. It was well past office hours, nearly midnight. He went to check it out and came back with a huge, white box tied with a red ribbon.

"It has your name on it," he said, handing me the card.

Isabel,

I hope it's not too small. It's hard to judge size on someone so much shorter than I am.

See you next week.

~Mercy

I frowned. Shane took the card from me and laughed. I took the box, touching it with only the tips of my fingers.

"It's not a grenade, Isabel. Just open it."

Pushing the stack of papers aside, I set it on the desk and tugged the bow, mumbling, "It could be a grenade. Or a severed head or something."

The box practically fell open, revealing layers of crisp, honey-gold satin. With a gasp, I pulled the dress out and stood to hold it to my body. The bodice came down to an empire waist tied with a delicate crème-colored ribbon above a full skirt.

The sleeves were small puffs designed to fall almost off the shoulder and covered in sheer lace that matched the ribbon.

I ran my hand along the smooth gown. I hated Mercy with a burning passion, but I had to admit, she had great taste in dresses.

"It's amazing," was all I could say. And it was the God's honest truth.

"You'll look beautiful," Shane whispered.

Looking at his face, I was transported back to the day we picked out my wedding dress. I knew it was bad luck for him to see it before the wedding, but I'd never believed in superstitions.

Maybe I should have.

Then I remembered that the whole point of the stupid ball was to make Shane more a part of their family, and less a part of mine. I stuffed the dress hastily back into the box and tossed it aside.

"Whatever. Listen, I've been thinking. All the local vamps will be at this party, right?" He nodded, frowning. "Well, so the vamp from the car might be in the mix. I think we should take the opportunity to sniff around a bit."

He snorted. "Oh, that's punny."

I picked up the phone and hit number one on the speed dial.

A female voice with a thick Asian accent crackled through the receiver, "House of Noodles."

I proceeded to place my usual order of orange chicken, wontons, and lo mien. *Thank goodness for twenty-four hour delivery*, I thought as I hung up. It was then I noticed a light flashing on the machine. I'd been so distracted by the file Xavier had given us,

I'd forgotten to check it when we got back.

I hit the playback button.

"Isabel, it's your mother. *Again*. We're having a family dinner this Friday night to meet your sister's new boyfriend and you *will* be there. I think they might be getting serious. If only your father were still around to see it. I expect you've taken care of that thing we discussed, and I also expect you to be at the house at five PM sharp. No excuses."

Beep.

Well, it looked like I had plans tomorrow night after all.

Shane laughed a *you-are-so-screwed* laugh. I threw a pencil at him, which he caught with two fingers and launched skillfully back into the pencil cup. Huffing, I switched on my computer and took out the scrap of paper with Phoebe's would-be suitor's name on it. Pulling up the people search website, I typed in his info.

Duke Murdoch was a volunteer firefighter who'd moved to Charleston from Virginia after losing two friends in a terrible hunting accident. He had a clean driving record, no outstanding warrants, and had never declared bankruptcy. Duke looked like a solid guy. I switched off the monitor, content to give my mother the green light on Phoebe's new beau. With any luck, they'd settle down, spit out a kid or two, and get Mom off *my* back.

The doorbell rang, signaling the arrival of dinner.

I paid the delivery boy, and then brought the order into the kitchen. "Shane, I'm gonna need you to do me a favor."

"Forget it," he answered without hesitation.

"Hey! I'm doing this stupid ceremony for you. You owe me."

He sighed and rubbed his eyes. "Fine. What?"

"I need you to call me at six o'clock, make that quarter till six, tomorrow night."

"Ah, an escape clause." He nodded. "No problem."

"Thanks." I dove into my box of chicken.

"Whatever," he replied in a nearly perfect imitation of my earlier remark. "I'm going to go to bed. I need to get my beauty sleep."

"There aren't enough hours in the day," I joked.

"Ha-ha."

"I'm going to stay up for a while. I want to see if the number of the credit card they gave Lisa is in the file anywhere. If it is, I can put a trace on it, see if anything hits."

He nodded, chucked his empty paper cup into the trash, and headed upstairs.

I finished my chicken, grabbed a fresh cup of coffee, and sat back down at the computer.

The account number wasn't in the file, but there was a receipt from a motel that used the old card slides. Using that number, I called the company and got an e-mail of the recent charges. Lisa had used the card to pay for lunch with her sister, but that was the last charge. There was also no record of who'd ordered the card, but I did get the billing address. A law firm downtown.

Also in the file was an accounting of what Lisa was being paid and the reduction of debt owed by her husband. Almost every penny from her illicit activities was going to pay off a fifty-thousand-dollar debt Robert Welch owed to a bookie referred to only as 360.

I dug back into Robert Welch's police file. Robert worked as an accountant for the law firm of Morris, King, and Deford. The name seemed familiar. Flipping back to the file from Xavier, I discovered why—a memo regarding a potential client for Lisa, a Judge Harris. It suggested that compromising photographs of said judge might be helpful in passing state legislation regarding a vampire registry bill, one of the many ideas circulating in congress.

The memo was on Morris, King, and Deford stationery. And the icing on the cake? Lisa's credit card bills were being sent to M, K, and D.

A quick search confirmed the Council had ties inside the law firm, so many in fact, that I was beginning to believe the entire firm was a front for Council activities. I'd always believed that lawyers were blood-sucking demons. Now I had proof.

So Robert was working for the company responsible for coercing his wife into a life of prostitution. His alibi for the time she went missing was airtight. But was that by design? I was beginning to suspect that the grieving husband knew more than he was admitting.

CHAPTER 8

Before I even opened the door to my childhood home, I could smell Mom's homemade lasagna. The house was a modest one, by Charleston standards at least, two stories tall with gray-and-white siding and a burgundy door. It had nothing on the massive, old plantation houses or the towering homes in the downtown area where I lived. My parents lived a few miles outside of town in a place called Ridgeville. Out in the boonies, my mother always joked. It wasn't that far from the truth. The yard was enormous, five acres fenced in, the only opening a large, iron gate at the head of the driveway that opened by electronic keypad. It was the home my great-grandparents had moved into just before they died, and it'd been in the family ever since. My Great-Grandpa Thaddeus hadn't been rich by any means, but his wise investments had bought this house and still managed to bring in enough, when combined with my father's pension, to at least pay the taxes and monthly utilities.

I'd barely stepped over the threshold when

my younger sister Sarah launched herself at me, wrapping me in an enthusiastic hug. I squeezed back, grateful that her time at UCLA had left her exterior, at least, unchanged. In a family full of dark-haired, short-ish Italian women, Sarah looked out of place. Thin, straight, strawberry-blonde hair was twisted into a bun at the crown of her head. Even without makeup, her face was flawless and pale, compared to her light blue eyes. When we'd been little, I'd teased her that she was adopted. Sarah had cried for hours. So did I... after my dad got through tanning my hide for it.

"When did your flight get in?" I asked as I squeezed my little sister.

"This morning." Clinging to me, she whispered, "Please help me," into my ear.

I rolled my eyes. *Mom must be in one of her moods again.*

"Sarah," Mom called from the kitchen, "run and get the good salad forks out of the china hutch, will you, dear?"

"Sure thing, Ma," she called back. Turning to me, she confided in hushed tones, "Mom hasn't shut up for five seconds, and I think Phoebe is about to go postal with the salad chopper."

I winked. "Don't worry, as soon as she sees me, she'll forget all about you guys and go into her 'my poor spinster daughter' number."

Sarah nodded, a bright smile spreading across her face. "Thanks, Isabel. I've missed you, ya know."

"Yeah. Same here, Shorty." I smiled back though Sarah had been taller than I had since eighth grade. "Now go get those forks before Mom calls in the

National Guard."

My mother's kitchen was exactly how it'd been since I was a toddler. The stark white cabinets locked it into a 1980-esque theme, which my mother had only exaggerated by choosing to decorate with gaudy, fake greenery. The whole room was littered with grape vines, pictures of grape vines, and towels, rags, and oven mitts with you guessed it—grape vines on them. Mom liked themes. And wine.

Mostly wine.

When I pushed open the door, she was bending over the stove, commenting on the bread sticks as Phoebe stood over the sink slicing carrots with more force than was completely necessary. When she saw me, Phoebe smirked.

"Hey Isabel. Glad you could make it." She tossed the abused carrots into a big salad bowl.

Mom looked over her shoulder at me before sliding the pan of bread out of the oven and onto the top of the stove. "Only twenty minutes late," she scolded in her typical passive-aggressive tone.

I shrugged, picking a piece of cucumber out of the salad and popping it into my mouth. Like lightning, Mom reached over and slapped my hand with a wooden spoon.

"Ow," I mumbled around the food in my mouth.

"You weren't raised by wolves. Wait 'til dinner." Then she turned on Phoebe, who was trying not to laugh. "And you, why don't you make the bruschetta? Actually, wait." She paused, looking over Phoebe like she was a cut of lamb at the supermarket and Mom was trying to judge her freshness. "Better yet, why don't you go put on some makeup? Blush, I think. You look a bit pale. And change your shirt. Pink really isn't your color, dear. Isabel, you can make the bruschetta, if you remember how."

I silently counted to five. "Yes, Mother, I remember how."

"Good." Handing me the basket of tomatoes, she pointed toward the cutting block.

As soon as Phoebe was out of the line of fire, I started talking. "So, I did that thing you wanted. Duke is squeaky clean. No red flags."

"Good. Thank you for checking for me. It's such a dangerous world we live in nowadays. I feel so... vulnerable without your father here to keep an eye on you girls."

I stopped chopping. "Yeah. I miss Dad, too."

"Well, you girls have always been two handfuls, all of you. I mean, look at Phoebe. Twenty years old and still hasn't had one stable relationship. I was beginning to worry she'd end up..." Mom trailed off.

It wasn't hard to fill in the blank.

"Like me?"

"I was going to say *alone*, but since you brought it up, yes. I worry about you, Isabel. You can't keep clinging to Shane. That ship has sailed. You need to move on, meet new people. Have you considered online dating? Suzanne Wheeler's daughter found a very nice young man that way."

"Really? He didn't, like, want to wear her skin as a suit or anything?"

Mom stopped what she was doing, put her hands on her hips, and glared at me. "It wouldn't kill you to try to meet someone."

"It might, in fact," I mutter, calling to mind

some news story about a man taking a lady he'd met online to Mexico and telling the police she's been eaten by alligators or something. "Besides, I work a lot. I have to, remember? Sarah's college isn't going to pay for itself."

That sounded harsher than I'd intended. Mom didn't say anything for a minute, which told me I'd scraped a nerve. I opened my mouth to apologize, but she cut me off.

"You work a lot. Yes, I'm aware of that. And I appreciate you doing it. I'm not heartless. I know you gave up quite a bit to come home and take over the business. But you don't have to work every minute. Surely, you've met some suitable prospects."

Prospects. Like men were gold nuggets to be panned out of the river.

"I meet plenty of men." I shrugged. "Most are criminals or adulterers, but I suppose I could bring one of them home."

She slapped me with the spoon again, this time across the shoulder. "Don't give me lip, girl," she ordered, expression stern. "This is not a joke. You don't want to spend your life alone."

I rolled my eyes and resumed chopping, garlic this time. "Ma, I'm far from an old maid."

At that minute, Phoebe walked into the kitchen wearing a clingy, lightweight sweater that accentuated her, ah, assets nicely. I whistled. Mom frowned and motioned to the stairs with her spoon.

"Phoebe! Go find something else to wear. That's barely decent and not appropriate for a family dinner." Phoebe rolled her eyes but turned to obey. Before she could step foot out of the door, Mom called out to her. "Remember, dear, no man is gonna buy the cow if he can get the milk for free!"

"Ma!" I chastised.

She looked at me flatly. "What?"

I blinked. "Did you just call Phoebe a cow?"

The doorbell rang at exactly seven. Phoebe had changed into a Mom-approved yellow blouse and tan slacks. Silently, we took up our usual positions in the hallway. Phoebe at the door, Sarah in front of me, and Mom at my back. It was the Stone family gauntlet. The only thing missing was Dad at the end.

Phoebe greeted Mathew with a quick peck on the cheek and led him in to be introduced to the firing squad, AKA Mom.

Duke was easily a half a foot taller than all of us, except for Sarah. Which meant he wasn't super tall for a man. He was muscular in the way that was more physical labor and less time in the gym. When we sat down for dinner, he pulled out Phoebe's chair, earning him a sly smile from Mother. But it wasn't long before the polite banter wore off and Mom went into full-blown inquisition mode.

"So, Duke, do you plan to continue your job as a firefighter after you get married?"

Sarah paled. Phoebe coughed and kicked me under the table. I grunted as she glared at me. Hey, what was I supposed to do about it?

"Yes, ma'am."

"Don't you think it's a bit dangerous?"

"No more so than most careers, ma'am," he

answered, far more politely than I would have.

"That's true," I interjected. "Just yesterday, I was in this dark basement with these two vampires and—"

Mom cut me off with, "That's nice, dear," before turning back to her prey. "And what about your family, Duke?

He looked to Phoebe, who turned to me. I shrugged.

"What about them?" He swallowed a bite of bread.

"Well, are they all well? What I mean is—are there any unfortunate genetic conditions in your family medical history?"

At that, I laughed so hard that red wine shot out my nose. Luckily, I had my napkin over my face. This was actually a standard Mom question. For her, boyfriends were nothing more or less than potential breeding stock.

I remembered the first time she'd met Shane and asked him the same thing. He'd responded that the only unfortunate genetic conditions were his Uncle Peter, who was a sword swallower in the traveling circus and his Aunt Bernie, the bearded lady. Mom's eye had twitched, but Dad had laughed his ass off and promptly told Mom to leave the boy alone.

Duke wasn't going to get so lucky. He sort of sat there with his mouth open, a bite of food falling off his raised fork.

"Mom, that's enough." I turned to Duke. "You'll have to excuse her. Her brain-to-mouth filter is in the shop."

Mom folded her arms across her chest. "Don't apologize for me. It's a legitimate question. Especially these days."

"What's that supposed to mean?" Phoebe finally piped up.

"I'm just being cautious."

"Ma, enough," I said sternly.

She shot me a look that clearly said, "We'll talk about this later," but she didn't push the subject.

Bless her heart, Sarah decided to break the tension. "So, what made you decide to become a firefighter?" she asked pleasantly.

"Well..." Duke smiled, and a dimple appeared to the left of his mouth. "I was living in New York, and I'd just started law school. One night, some of my friends and I went to this club inside this old warehouse. Somehow, a fire broke out. I got out all right, but one of my friends was trapped inside. The firemen got there and got everybody out, but it was too late for my buddy. That's when I decided to change paths. I wanted to do something important, something that would really help people."

By the end of his tale, Mom was looking at Duke like he'd personally hung the moon. With a beaming smile, she offered him another slice of bread.

I rolled my eyes. Before I could think of something to say, my phone rang.

"Is that the theme song from *Buffy the Vampire Slayer*?" Sarah asked seriously.

I nodded. "Yeah. You know how it is. If I can't laugh about my ex-fiancé being turned into a bloodsucker, then who can?"

I shot my mother an apologetic look and flipped

open the phone, sliding my chair back from the table.

"Hey. This is your escape call."

I could tell from the tone of Shane's voice that something was wrong.

"What's the matter?" I asked, still in earshot of Mom, who was now glaring at me.

"I'm just... tired," he said as if trying to decide if that were the right word.

I raised my voice just an octave and continued my "conversation."

"Are you sure this can't wait 'til tomorrow?" I pulled the phone away from my head and mouthed, *I'm Sorry*, to my mother. "Yeah, I'll be there in ten..." I trailed off, surprised by a knock at the door.

"If that's you, Shane, I'm gonna..." I whispered sharply, making my way to the front of the house, holding the phone at my side as I pulled the door open.

My sister Heather stepped inside. She wore a flowing, blue sundress and matching headscarf. She was layered with so much jewelry and bangles she looked like a gypsy.

"Hey, sis! Did ya miss me?"

I put the phone back to my head. "Um, Shane, I'm gonna have to call you back."

"Who was at the door?" Mom asked as I slipped back into the dining room.

"A bunch of Girl Scouts with torches and pitchforks," I joked half-heartedly. "Said something about you owing them money."

From behind me, Heather popped out and yelled, "Surprise!"

Mom practically launched from her chair and rushed to hug her in a vice grip. "Heather, oh my heavens! I'm so glad you're home."

"It's good to see you too, Mom." She smiled, pulled away, and asked with a light laugh, "Do you have room for one more at the table?"

Sarah stood up and gave our youngest sister a hug. "Where have you been, brat?"

"Oh, you know." Heather waved her hand. "Here and there. Traveling, learning, studying the universe."

"Like, physics?" I asked. "Or getting high in an observatory?"

"You can take Isabel's place," Mom interjected as she filled a plate of food. "She was just leaving."

"Forget it." I sat back down. "This meal just got interesting."

"What about Shane?" Phoebe laughed.

I blew a raspberry at her.

"Not at the table," Mom snapped.

Heather pulled out the empty chair at the end of the table and sat down.

"You look like Esmeralda from the *Hunchback of Notre Dame,*" Sarah joked.

Sarah was right. Heather's curly hair was long and disheveled, held at bay only by a scrap of blue cloth. Every finger on her hand had a ring on it, and she'd ditched her eyebrow stud for a Bindi jewel in the middle of her forehead.

"I've been studying with some monks in Bali.

It's so amazing over there. You wouldn't believe it." She smiled as Mom set a full plate in front of her. Heather looked at it, smiled awkwardly, and pushed it away. "Sorry. I should have mentioned that I no longer eat the flesh of other creatures. Bad karma."

Mom's eye twitched. I tried really hard not to laugh. Sarah just stared at her.

"So, what brings you back to this end of the planet?" Phoebe asked.

"Well," Heather leaned forward, "I was in this meditative trance and... I had a vision."

I snickered, Sarah snorted, and Phoebe looked at her like she was nuts. Then, in slow-motion unison, we turned to Mom, whose smile was cracking around the edges.

Phoebe patted Duke's hand. "Maybe we should get going."

As if realizing for the first time that Duke was still in the room, Mom motioned to him. "Pardon my manners. Duke, this is my youngest daughter, Heather. Heather, this is Duke, Phoebe's friend."

Heather stood and grasped his hand across the table, not just shaking it, but covering it with her other hand as well. She smiled. "Oh, yes. I saw you in my vision. It's nice to meet you in person."

If Duke was uncomfortable, he hid it really well, just smiling and nodding. *Hey, he might just make it in the family after all.*

Mom got up slowly and walked Phoebe and Duke to the door.

As soon as she was out of earshot, I leaned forward. "Heather, are you *trying* to give Mom a stroke?"

"What do you mean?" Her face looked pleasantly blank.

"Um, hello? What's with all the psychic stuff?" Sarah chimed in. "And a vegetarian? Have you lost your mind? We eat bacon-stuffed turkey for Thanksgiving."

After a brief pause and a strange wave of her arms, Heather replied, "I've been on a path to enlightenment. And on my journey, I've made some important discoveries about myself. I understand your reluctance to see me as the grown woman I am now, but you'll come to accept the new me."

"The woman you've become?" I snorted. "Heather, you're eighteen, and you're an idiot."

She was unfazed, responding simply, "I've had a spiritual experience."

"Did it involve drinking the Kool-Aid?" I asked sarcastically.

"Isabel, maybe you should go," Sarah said, trying to sound diplomatic.

I shook my head, folding my hands across my chest. "Forget it. For once, I'm not the biggest target on Mom's dartboard. I wanna stick around to watch this."

As if on cue, Mom came back in the dining room. Painting a smile on her face, she walked over to Heather. "If you're hungry I'm sure I could whip you up something, meat free."

I straightened. "What? She comes home after running away at sixteen, declares that she's a vegetarian *and* a psychic, and she gets offered a meal?" I sank back in my chair. "This is so unfair."

Mom shot me a look, and then snapped, "Isabel,

why don't you head home? It sounded like Shane really needed something."

"I... what? I'm being kicked out? But she—"

"Don't be such a drama queen," Mom ordered.

I shook my head, sliding my chair away from the table as I muttered, "Fine. Whatever. You guys have fun catching up. I have work to do anyway."

Mom headed for the kitchen.

Heather came over and put her arms around me for a hug. "It is really good to see you again, Isabel. I'll come by soon to catch up."

I swallowed. "Sounds good. But Heather..." I pulled back, looking her in the eye. "If this is about money, don't go to Mom with it. Come talk to me. She's barely squeaking by as it is."

She smiled and shook her head. "Don't worry about that, silly."

I stepped out onto the porch and turned to walk away before she added, "But you probably *should* be worried about Phoebe's boyfriend being a werewolf."

Heather smiled and slammed the door in my face.

CHAPTER 9

Stunned by Heather's abrupt declaration, I slid into my car, resting my head on the steering wheel as a headache grew behind my eyes. Was she right about the brave Duke? I mean, I didn't particularly like the idea of my little sister being involved with one of the furry persuasion. Was that speciest of me? Maybe. And besides, who was I to judge? I had a vampire shacking up in my attic after all. I sighed as my purse vibrated a second before busting out with the *Buffy* tune.

Grumpy, I flipped open the phone. "What, Shane?"

"Izzy, I think you need to come home. Now."

Behind the tense voice, I could make out sirens. "What? What happened?" I hurriedly slipped the key in the ignition and turned, suddenly impatient for the engine to come roaring to life.

"We have a problem. The police are here. Just... just get here. Now." *Click.*

"Shane?" I asked into the receiver, but he was gone. I flipped the phone closed and tossed it into the seat next to me, mumbling, "Great."

Peeling out of my mom's driveway I sped home, hoping the police were there to help Shane with whatever had happened and not to carry him off to jail.

After cursing my way through five red lights and three stop signs, I saw the cruisers' flashing red and blue lights before I turned onto my street. When I pulled up to the curb in front of my house, the first thing I noticed was the yellow crime scene tape strung across my porch. Second, I noticed Shane and Mercy standing in the side yard, talking to Reggie. Neither vampire was in handcuffs or perma-dead, so that was a relief.

Shane must have heard my door slam because he said something to Mercy and Reggie and walked toward me. But knowing he was safe, my interest was focused on the black bag lying across my porch.

"Isabel." Shane put his arm around my shoulders.

"What happened?" I nodded toward the porch. "Who's in the bag?"

At that moment, Reggie and Mercy joined us. She slid her head under Shane's other arm in a maneuver that was both possessive and childish. I shook my head and slid out of Shane's grasp.

Reggie answered my question. "Shane and Miss Mercy here say they came home from a movie and found the deceased on your porch. He's been identified as one Billy Young."

"Wait. Young, the arsonist?"

"Looks that way. You tell anyone else that he was bothering you, Isabel?"

I shook my head, staring at the bag, trying to

make sense of the situation. On the one hand, I was weak with relief that it hadn't been someone I cared about. On the other, I was racking my brain. Who would have done this? "Just Shane," I replied automatically.

Reggie nodded. "It looks as if he was killed somewhere else and placed here."

"How do you know?" I asked.

"The body was drained of blood. But there isn't a drop here." He motioned toward the ground.

"So, you're thinking vampire?" I asked.

Reggie shrugged. "Maybe, but there were no bite marks. It looks like whoever did the deed slit the bastard's throat."

Shane and I exchanged a glance. It didn't sound like a vamp kill, but it didn't exclude them either. A squeal of tires from behind me made me turn. A Channel 7 news van had just showed up to the party. *Super*.

Reggie tucked his notebook in his pocket and nodded. "If y'all will excuse me, I need to go deal with this."

As soon as he was out of earshot, Shane grabbed me by the elbow and led me off to the side, Mercy still in tow.

"That isn't all," he said in hushed tones. "When we found him, there was a big red bow on his head and a tag stuck to his shirt. Isabel, it had your name on it."

"My name? Anything else?"

He shook his head.

"We, uh, left the bow, but I took the tag before the cops got here. I was afraid they might think..."

"That I had something to do with the murder," I added softly.

Shane's heart was in the right place, but if the cops ever found out he'd tampered with the evidence, he and Mercy could both be screwed.

"Exactly."

"What kind of deranged person would put a bow and a tag on a dead body?" I asked out loud. To my surprise, Mercy answered.

"Someone who was leaving you a gift," she said in her usual over-the-top accent. With a petulant frown, she added quietly, "She gets the best presents." Louder, she said, "Oh, Shane, can we go now? All these sirens are giving me a headache."

He looked surprised at her request. "Oh, well, I don't know," he said gently. "I don't think Isabel should be alone tonight."

Mercy shot me a look so dirty it could have lit me on fire.

The catty, insecure part of me wanted to play the frightened victim who needed him to stay, but the truth was, I'd have rather eaten glass than admit any weakness in front of that woman. The competitive side won out. What could I say? I sucked at damsel in distress.

"Nah, I'm fine. Really. I'm just gonna grab a shower and hit the sack," I lied smoothly, knowing full well I'd never be able to get to sleep after this.

Shane looked at me like I was full of shit, but he didn't challenge me. A lingering, vulnerable part of me was disappointed.

"All right then. Come on, Mercy. Let's go."

It took another hour before I'd answered all the

cops' questions and the coroner had taken the body. Reggie stayed with me and did a walk-through of the house just to make sure no one was inside and nothing had been stolen. Near as we could tell, whoever left the body had never made it inside. Unfortunately, that did little to calm my nerves.

I did everything I could to avoid going to bed. I sent some e-mails that were sitting in my outbox, returned a frantic call from my mother who'd seen the entire thing on the ten o'clock news, scrubbed my bathtub until I had a contact high from the cleaners, and then I watched *Avatar*.

My nerves finally settled down just as first light crept into my windows. Something about dawn made me feel safer, despite the fact that Shane still hadn't made it home. *He was probably shacking up with Mercy somewhere,* I told myself grumpily as I slid into my cool bed and closed my eyes.

The cell phone in my nightstand started ringing just after I'd hit the sack, or at least, that was how it felt.

Peeling my eyes open, I glanced at the numbers on the glowing clock face. 6:48. I'd been in bed less than an hour. The vibrating ring tone told me it was Shane. I snatched the phone off the table and chucked it full force at the far wall. It collided with a satisfying crack, falling to the floor. Silent.

If people are going to insist on calling me before seven AM, I'm gonna need a cell phone that can handle being thrown across the room. I thought with some venom. *Can you hear me now?*

Making a mental note to swing by the electronics

store later, feeling grateful I'd taken out the extra insurance this time, I tucked my head under the pillow, cocooned in my blankets, and drifted back to sleep.

It was almost three in the afternoon when I finally woke up. One of the major downsides of having a semi-nocturnal partner was it made keeping unusual business hours and existing on little-to-no sleep job requirements.

Dressing quickly I headed down to the office to boot up the computer. The red button on the answering machine blinked angrily at me. I hit the button with the eraser of my pencil, and the speakers crackled to life.

"You have three new messages. First message."

Shane's voice. "Hey Isabel. Just calling to check in. I found out something interesting you're gonna want to hear."

Sighing, I leaned back in my chair.

Beep.

"Ms. Stone, this is Mr. Curtis. I was just checking in to see how you were progressing with the case. Please give me a call."

I pulled out the Curtis file and found his number. Figuring he was probably still at work, I decided to call his house and leave a message. At some point, I was going to have to reveal what I'd discovered about his daughter's dirty little secret, but until I knew for sure how the vamps fit into the equation, I'd play that card close to the vest.

Beep.

"Hey Isabel. It's Heather. I was hoping we could get together for lunch this week. I have some stuff to share with you. It's not exactly urgent, but it's important, okay? So call me. Or I'll call you back later. Whichever. *Ciao, chica!*"

Rolling my eyes, I hit the delete button on the machine and dialed Mr. Curtis. As expected, I got his machine.

"Hello, this is Isabel. I wanted to call and let you know that I have a new lead in your daughter's case. However, it's too soon to tell whether it will pan out. I should have more solid answers for you by next week. I'm doing everything I can. I'll be in touch."

No, that wasn't going to be a pleasant conversation at all. Hopefully, I'd be able to go to him with something other than his daughter's shady past and give the poor man some answers. Turning to the computer, I pulled up my online calendar. Shane's vamp cotillion was tomorrow night, which was good and bad. *Mostly bad*, I thought, biting my lower lip.

As much as I was ready to get some answers on this case, part of me really wasn't ready to let him go. Selfish, I knew, but that was just how I felt. For so long, he'd been *my* Shane. Even after we weren't involved romantically anymore, he was still such a huge part of me. I didn't want to admit it—I'd rather have eaten glass than confessed this to anyone—but deep down, I always hoped we'd end up together. I shook my head. It was silly. Insane, actually. Him being what he was meant we could never have a life together, not the life I wanted anyway.

But there was a part of me that still longed for the happily ever after that he'd promised me once. We'd been so close to perfect. So close to forever.

But joining the Conclave meant, at a minimum, he'd have to move out. They liked to keep the neonates close to the nest. They probably wouldn't let him continue to work with me, either. They'd give him some cushy job at one of their many businesses, all the better to keep an eye on him. The moment they took him in, he'd become an *investment*. And they expected returns on their investments. It wasn't an arrangement I'd ever agree to, but at the end of the day, it wasn't my decision. Sure, I'd put on big-girl panties and deal with it, but it still made my heart hurt.

Snapping myself out of the gloomy thoughts, I dialed my mother's house. Heather picked up on the first ring.

"Hey, sis," she answered with no prelude.

"Hi, Heather. Listen. I got your message. Lunch doesn't work for me, but how about an early dinner? Like around five?"

On the other end of the phone, she chortled. "Sure, we could hit the early-bird dinner at the senior center."

"Ha-ha."

"Naw, five is fine. How about we meet at *Muse*, you know, down on Society Street?"

I rolled my eyes. I'd been hoping for beer and hot dogs. She wanted an upscale French wine bar. Figured.

"Sure. *Muse* it is. See you at five," I said and hung up.

Much as I was loathe to admit it, Heather seemed like a different person than the bratty little sister I'd grown up with. As crazy as she sounded, she had a stillness to her, like she was finally comfortable in her own skin. It couldn't have been easy being the baby in a family like ours. By the time Heather was a teenager, Mom was busy with the bakery, Dad worked all the time, and the rest of us were too busy getting our own lives started to take any real notice of her. I pinched the bridge of my nose, squeezing my eyes closed. We were pretty lucky she turned out as well as she did, all things considered. Although it'd almost killed Mom when she took off, maybe she really did find herself out there in the world. The jury was still out on that one. But now that she was home, I just couldn't help wondering why.

Something in the pit of my stomach told me that my baby sister was going to make me pay for this dinner, in more ways than one.

In the chaos of the night before, I'd nearly forgotten the accusation Heather had made about Phoebe's new boyfriend. I'd done a preliminary background check on the guy at Mom's insistence, but there hadn't been anything to suggest he was a *were*. I decided, on the off chance that Heather was right somehow, to dig just a little deeper.

It wasn't like the *weres* were obvious about what they were. They were the most secretive of all supernatural beings. Hell, who could blame them? When the vamps first debuted to the world, they'd been all but branded and sent to prison camps. According to Dad's files, dozens of vamps were rounded up and put in camps all over the country. But something amazing happened. The vampires *let* people do it. They didn't retaliate or fight back, and on the rare occasion when one did go postal, he or she was dealt with quickly and decisively by the others. It was that more than anything that made people start to see them less as monsters and more as people.

It was a brilliant strategy, very Gandhi. Almost overnight, they went from dangerous predators to a piteous, oppressed, misunderstood minority group.

However, there were limitations to people's generosity. It was illegal for vampires to work in certain professions, such as teaching, medicine, things like that, which was why Shane had been canned from his job as a middle school teacher after the change. Vampires were required to register with the state like sex offenders, and they weren't allowed to vote. It was like, welcome to the 1800s. Err, I guessed for some of them, it would be 'welcome back'.

Still, they had at least won a few key battles. They were guaranteed basic protection under the law, which meant that you couldn't just kill them on sight. And the laws were constantly in flux. Elected officials argued weekly about whatever new scrap of legislation was on the table, everything from inheritance taxes and property restrictions to basic human rights and equal opportunity issues. Currently, vampires had the right to an attorney, trial, etc. Unless they were *seen* killing a human. For a vampire, murder was punishable by immediate execution. No jury, no sitting in a cell for years working on appeals. Just instant, fiery death.

Who could blame *weres* for worrying that

they'd be treated the same?

The bad blood between the vamps and *weres* went way back. From what Shane told me, it basically boiled down to early territory disputes that led to bloody battles. The fact that Xavier had them working side by side here in Charleston, well, that was an oddity of epic proportions.

The way my father described them was as warring factions. Neither remembered who fired the first shot, but each was determined to fire the last. He also warned that *were* pack politics were bloody, archaic, and should be avoided at all costs. Dad also named a man he believed to be the pack Alpha, the leader. But that file was put together in the late sixties. No other mention was made of the furry community.

It took nearly an hour of scanning newspaper archives from Duke's hometown before I found what I was looking for. An article describing a bear attack on an adolescent boy during a hunting trip.

According to the article, Duke and his father, Martin, had been elk hunting when Duke had been attacked by a bear. His father managed to frighten the animal off, but Duke was seriously injured. The bear was never found. I scanned the archives further, but there was no follow-up on the incident.

I leaned back in my chair, folding my arms across my chest as I stared at the picture frozen on my screen of a young Duke being carted off in an ambulance.

Okay, it didn't prove anything, but the coincidence was too big to be ignored. I'd have a talk with Heather tonight, try to figure out where she'd come up with the accusation, and then do what I did best.

Get some answers.

CHAPTER 10

Inever returned Shane's call, which wasn't deliberate, just an oversight on my part. That didn't stop him from tracking me down like a truancy officer on crack. I had just pulled up outside the *Katz Lair*, a strip club near the old naval base that I knew for a fact was owned by one of Xavier's shell companies.

Vamps had their fingers in all kinds of pies in Charleston, from the biggest banks and mortgage companies, real estate firms, and even medical labs, to the shady underbelly of Charleston nightlife. Bars, strip clubs, a couple of porn shops. But then, they'd had centuries to horde enough cash to buy their way into just about whatever they wanted.

"Filling out an application?" Shane asked flippantly as he opened my car door, scaring the bejeezus out of me as I reached for the handle.

"You know me, always looking to expand my horizons," I snarked back, slipping out of the car.

My boots clacked across the pavement as I turned my back to Shane and walked toward the glowing neon sign hanging over the nondescript front door. Except for the tall, bald man standing there with his hands clasped in front of him, which made him look like a wannabe Secret Service agent/ Hell's Angel, the parking lot was empty. A few barren cars dotted the lot, but there were no other signs of life.

Shane slammed the car door and jogged to catch up with me, grabbing my arm and pulling me to a stop. He leaned down to bring his face level with mine. "Seriously, what are we doing here?"

I pulled my arm out of his hand. "I'm going to go in there to see if I can talk to some of the girls, find out if anyone knows anything about this prostitution ring the victim was involved in."

"So, your plan is to walk into a known vampire club and start asking questions? Solid."

I turned away from the door and lowered my voice. "Look, I know this is one of Xavier's clubs. I didn't call you because I get that you can't be involved in something like this. Okay? I'm not trying to piss in your Wheaties here, but I need some answers. So far, the only person who's been able to provide them is Xavier. So just go back to the house and wait for me there."

I spun on my heel with the intention of leaving him standing there. Okay, so I was still a little bit bitter about the whole ditching me for Mercy thing, but my point was still a valid one. Shane had been my wingman for months and it'd been great, but he was about to be planted firmly on enemy territory, and I had to get used to doing things on my own.

When I reached the door, however, I wasn't

alone. I could practically feel Shane standing behind me, his cool breath on the back of my neck.

"Club doesn't open 'til seven," the bouncer said, expression stoic.

"I'm here to apply for a job." I flashed my best sultry smile.

The big man looked me over quickly. I'd opted for a shock-and-awe campaign, so I'd worn my best soft leather pants in jet black and matching faux-corset top. I looked badass and felt like S&M Barbie.

He raised one eyebrow.

Behind me, Shane sighed. "She's kidding. We're here to see Xavier. He in?"

"Not yet." The bouncer pushed the door open anyway. "You can wait in his office."

I muttered thanks and stepped past him.

The club wasn't what I'd expected. I wasn't ashamed to admit my particular field of business took me into the occasional den of iniquity, and they were all pretty much the same. Mirrored walls and ceilings, gleaming brass poles, flashing colored lights, dark corners, and glitter every-freaking-where. But this place? This place looked like the *Taj Mahal*.

The *Katz Lair* had a distinctly Arabian Nights theme going. The walls were hung with sheer, gauzy fabrics in an array of bright reds and purples. The floor was gold, not real gold of course, but the kind of color real gold should be. The bar was a solid piece of onyx with jewels inlaid along the edge, and the stage was round, poleless, and surrounded by empty gold chairs that looked like mini-thrones.

Trying really hard not to be impressed with the

joint, I sashayed up to the bar. Now, as a rule, I was against women who liked to play stupid or flaunt their assets to get attention, but this was legitimate strategy on my part. The men who worked in places like this tended to buy into the female sex-kitten stereotype. Playing into that stereotype would allow me to sort of fly under their radar. People were less threatened by—less suspicious of—things they considered the norm. It would give me the element of surprise, should the need arise.

I really hoped it wouldn't arise.

I smiled sweetly at the man behind the counter. "Hi. I'm looking for Xavier. The guy outside said we could wait in his office."

He was olive skinned with tight brown curls in his hair. Not black exactly, but definitely some flavor other than vanilla. He looked past me to Shane. I watched in the mirror that ran behind the bar as Shane smiled, flashing fang.

The bartender nodded toward the back of the building, behind the stage to where a row of what looked like one-way mirrors stood elevated over the entire floor.

"Second door on the right," he said, towel drying the counter.

Shane nodded, and I winked in thanks.

As it turned out, while the club itself was beautiful, it had nothing on Xavier's personal office.

The room wasn't large, but it was impeccably clean. A brown leather couch on one side of the room looked out onto the stage area, and a large, white, granite-top desk dominated the center of the room. It was almost crescent-moon shaped, with a high-back leather chair tucked behind it. A slim laptop computer sat black screened on the desk next to a cut-crystal vase full of tall, red flowers that looked exotic and possibly carnivorous. There were no papers, no clutter for me to sift through as we waited. Not a single pen or paperclip. The urge to go rifle through the drawers taunted me. A quick glance around put the kibosh to that though. In two corners were small, discreet video cameras, red lights blinking.

"Smile, Shane, we're on *Candid Camera*." I waved to the one-eyed surveillance equipment.

Shane stood unmoving in front of the one-way glass, watching the nearly empty room below us. I slid onto the cushy sofa. It was softer than it looked, almost as soft as my pants, which was saying something.

"We need one of these for the office," I muttered absently, stroking the arm.

Shane snorted. "Yeah. Someday when you land a millionaire client and don't have to hand the check over to your mother."

I swallowed. He had a point, but it was still a crappy thing to say. I bit my tongue, understanding that he'd put himself in a tricky situation coming here to back me up like this. But I didn't want to discuss personal issues in front of whoever was on the other side of those cameras.

"Maybe I just need to find myself a rich husband like Mom keeps saying," I joked.

A moment passed before he answered, his voice barely a whisper. "I'll be rich soon."

He was right, technically, but hearing him say it

out loud still stunned me. Being part of the vampire community came with perks, and disposable cash was one of them. The vamps in charge considered it an investment in loyalty. Like the Mafia, they were pretty charitable with the cash, but then you owed them. Like *forever*.

Most vamps were chosen to be turned, and they could afford to be picky with their recruits. Everybody was chosen for a reason. Some because of their connections, status, or wealth—some because they were artisans or tech-heads. Whatever the coalition needed at the time or was thought to be valuable enough to preserve.

Shane, being changed without permission by a rogue, hadn't been chosen. He was clawing his way into society the hard way, and we both knew that at some point, his loyalty to them would be tested. It was a test he had to pass, or he would die. For realsies this time.

"You offering yourself up, Brooks?" I asked playfully, trying to break the tension that had his face too stern, his shoulders too tight.

He didn't answer for a minute, and I was afraid I'd offended him. Then he turned to me, smiling.

"Yeah. 'Cause that worked out so well the first time."

I only half-laughed. His words were like a knife in my heart, though I'd never let him see the cut.

Shane opened his mouth to say something else, but he stopped short when the door to the office was flung open and Xavier strode in. In an instant, the entire room was transformed. The air was suddenly thicker, the smell of him, rich and dark like amber, wafted around me. I let myself breath it in, trying to slow my rapidly jumping heart.

Even in jeans and a T-shirt, he'd look like he was wearing a tux, I thought appreciatively. It was just something in the way he carried himself, always so formal. Today, he wore a navy blue suit with subtle pinstripes and a crème-colored, button-down shirt. He didn't seem to notice us, as in one smooth motion, he slipped off his jacket and hung it on the rack behind the door. He caught me looking him over and grinned. I shrugged, unashamed. Just because I wasn't ordering the meal didn't mean I couldn't look at the menu.

"What can I do for my favorite private detective this evening?" he asked, sitting down in his chair and flicking on his computer.

When I didn't answer, frankly because I wasn't sure if he was talking to Shane or me, he looked up, giving me a once over in return. He raised one dark eyebrow. "Come to audition, I hear?"

I snorted. "You wish."

Xavier's smile widened, one dimple appearing on the side of his face, and clasped his hands under his chin, waiting. It was a gesture that was both innocent and seductive, making my stomach knot involuntarily. It was all I could do not to melt into a puddle.

"I know that Lisa Welch was hooking for you guys. I was hoping you might be willing to help me get my hands on a list of her clients or at least speak to some of your dancers here, see if any of them knew anything."

Xavier put his hands down, the playful smile

fading from his face. "No, I'm afraid not. Bad for business, giving out my associates' information like that."

Shane remained silent.

I pressed on. "A woman is missing, probably dead."

"So you said." Xavier pulled open his bottom desk drawer, removing a pad of paper and mechanical pencil.

I sat back, folded my arms across my chest, and sighed. "Don't you care?"

"I care about *my* people, the vampires I'm sworn to protect. If it comes down to a choice between protecting them and helping you, well..."

My jaw clenched. *Damn vampires.* I stood, walking toward the desk where Xavier was scribbling absently on the piece of yellow paper.

"Did you kill her?"

He didn't look up. "No."

"Did one of your employees?"

"Not that I know of."

"How do I know you're telling me the truth?"

"You don't," he said flatly, still not looking up.

I put my palms flat on his desk and leaned forward. "Look, I know you don't care about the life of some human, but she had a husband, a family. They at least deserve to know what happened to her. Please," I added for good measure. "If you know anything that will help me give them some answers, a name, a place, anything. Please."

He stopped writing, tore the paper off the pad, and stood up, face to face with me, his hands covering mine. A tingle of electricity passed through

his skin, forcing a shiver deep into my body. I shook
it off, hard. Whatever vamp charm he was pulling
on me, I wasn't gonna let myself fall for it.

"If I could help you, Isabel, I would. Your father
was a good man. I know what you risked coming
to me, what you both risked." His eyes flashed to
Shane, and my heart sank into my stomach. "But
there is nothing else I can do."

He let me go and stepped back. "Believe it or
not, even I have to answer to someone."

He held my eyes, and I sucked in a surprised
breath as I realized what was happening.

Standing up, I nodded. "I understand. I won't
bother you again. Shane, let's go." Turning, I walked
to the door without waiting for my partner.

We were back in the parking lot before he
stopped me with a hand on my arm.

"*I won't bother you again*? What the hell?" He
pulled my eyelids back with his thumbs. "Who are
you and what did you do with Isabel?"

I slapped him. He stepped back, and I held out
my hand. In my palm rested the tiny, crumpled
piece of yellow notepaper.

"Oh."

"Yeah. Oh."

Without another word, we got in the car.

"Why do you think Xavier's helping us?" I finally
asked on the drive back to the house.

"I don't think he's helping us; I think he's helping
you," Shane said, carefully un-crumpling the paper.

"Because he was friends with my dad?" I
wondered out loud.

Shane snorted. "Yeah, right."

I looked at him quickly, and then back to the road. "What's that supposed to mean?"

"Nothing," Shane grumbled.

I rolled my eyes. Whatever. "What does it say?"

"It's an address and a time," he answered.

"What time?" I looked at the dashboard clock. It was just after four, nearly time to meet Heather for dinner.

"Midnight."

"What?" I asked, picking up the icy tone in his voice.

"And it says, *come alone.*"

CHAPTER 11

I played the scenario in my head, trying to figure out what angle Xavier was working. It was possible he didn't want it known that he was helping me. I could understand that. Even so, the cloak-and-dagger routine was just a little melodramatic for my taste.

Shane was in a mood when we got back to the house. He didn't have to say anything. His body language screamed at me not to go to the meeting. I knew I'd have been just as hesitant to let him do something like that alone. But he was moving out soon, cutting ties with me and the business. At some point, I'd have to go it alone and really, why postpone the inevitable?

So while he slammed drawers in the kitchen, I took the extra time to go over the case files again.

"Hey," I called across the house.

He walked in, nursing a mug of blood. "Yeah? What's up?"

I held up the case file. "Did Lisa's sister mention why nobody told the police about the husband's gambling problems?"

He nodded. "Said she was the only one who knew besides Lisa. Didn't tell the police because, well, she didn't want to accuse him. Also, she seemed pretty convinced that he didn't have anything to do with Lisa's disappearance."

"She's probably right, but just to cover our bases, do you think you could look into that angle?"

"You want me to talk to the local bookies, just try to follow the cash?"

I reached into my drawer and pulled out my new, slim-line tracking device. "Literally."

I handed him the microchip. It was no bigger than the tip of my finger and impressively thin. Nearly paper thin.

"You can pull out three hundred bucks from the business account. See if you can find the bookie Welch used, place a bet, and we can track the money back to the boss."

"Or I could just beat the information out of him," Shane offered, handing the tiny chip back to me.

"There you go again, ruining my fun."

He winked. "You're just mad because I make all your silly gadgets obsolete."

"Fine. Do it your way. But I'm not bailing you out of jail, *again*." I said with a huff.

After changing into something a little less combat ready, I headed for *Muse*.

The chichi restaurant was already filling up at ten after five, which was when my oh-so-punctual sister arrived. Her long dress was startlingly red and low cut. She looked more like a Hollywood starlet than a tree-hugging vegan.

"Thanks for meeting me." Heather flipped her dark brown hair over her shoulder.

How can we possibly be related? "Yeah, well, I have a few questions," I said as gently as I could under the circumstances.

She picked up the menu, blocking my eye contact with her. "Ask away."

I took a sip of my seven-dollar soda. "Fine. Let's start with, 'Where the hell have you been?' and work our way to 'What do you know about Phoebe's new boyfriend and how do you know it?'"

She put the menu down and folded her hands on top of it. "Well, I was traveling. You know, seeing the world."

"While you were seeing the world, Dad died," I blurted, more harshly than I'd intended. "Mom was devastated. We got left to pick up the pieces."

Heather frowned. "I know. I'm sorry about that. When I heard about Dad, I wanted to come straight home, but he was already gone, and I was having a really hard time. I was in a bad place for a while, sis."

"So were we."

"Yes. But I had to deal with it my way. If I'd come home then, I just would have made things worse. We both know that."

She was probably right. Still, that didn't make it okay.

The waiter made his way over.

"I'll have the tofu penne with the braised crème sauce, please," Heather ordered, handing over her menu. "And a glass of chardonnay. Thank you."

I blinked, still unprepared to order despite my

ten-minute head start on reading the menu. "Um, I'll have the Ahi. Thanks."

He took our menus and walked away without a word.

"And as for Duke," Heather continued, "it's pretty obvious, at least to those of us who are sensitive to that sort of thing."

"Explain," I demanded before taking a drink of water.

She sighed. "Well, I'm a little psychic, you see. I discovered it while I was in Virginia studying focus meditation with this yogi—"

"Focus," I said, cutting her off before she could get too far off track. "Duke."

"Right. Anyway, I can feel him. Or, well, the air around him. It's warmer than a regular human."

"The air?"

"Yeah. It's like, his aura burns hotter. I can sort of feel it. Not like a vampire. They don't actually have auras. Makes them pretty easy to spot, too."

Uh-huh.

"So, how have you been?" she asked with a smile. "Is it weird, living in Dad's old office? Are you planning to go back to school?"

I gaped at her. "I can't go back to school. Mom's bakery barely pays for itself, and Dad's life insurance only covered funeral expenses. Mom gets his pension, but I have to help pay for Sarah's tuition. UCLA is expensive. Add in the expenses around the office, and there isn't much left over."

"Well, I'm back now. I can help Mom out."

I cocked my head. Heather was planning to actually work? Was it Opposite Day? "What do you mean? You? Looking for a job?"

"Actually, I'm opening my own business." She gave me a 'don't-act-so-surprised' look.

Oh, that wasn't good. I could actually feel the verbal blow coming in the air. I carefully set the soda back on the table so I wouldn't lose my temper at whatever she was going to say next and end up with a fist full of broken glass.

"I'm going to open my own fortune-telling shop—with Tarot cards, tea leaves, and palm reading. I'll sell candles and oils, too. I know how to make the best patchouli oil..."

She kept talking but I quit listening, a subtle but painful throb developing behind my left eye.

"Where?" I asked when she stopped to take a breath.

"I have a little cash stocked away. I'm gonna buy a space down by the Old Slave Market. There's a place next to the Haunted Tours office for sale. It's the perfect location really—"

"Where did you get the money?"

She flicked her hair again. "Sold some stuff."

I raised an eyebrow. "What stuff?"

"Pirate gold. What does it matter? Point is, I'm making my dreams come true. And I'm happy to help Mom out with whatever I can. You know, once I get some steady business coming in."

There was so much I wanted to say, all of it bitchy and judgmental. I held it in, though I still couldn't manage the kind of wide-eyed enthusiasm she obviously had about the venture.

She was talking about furnishings when our meal came. I let her ramble on, chewing my food slowly. My mind was going back and forth between what I was going to do about her and what I was going to do about my meeting with Xavier that night. And wondering if I was going to get any more dead guys on my doorstep as gifts.

"Maybe I should get a dog," I interrupted, thinking out loud.

Heather laughed, taking a drink of her wine. "Why not? Phoebe did."

I decided to change the subject, once we stopped laughing, that was. "Okay Heather, spill it. Why the dinner invite?"

I took a drink of my soda as she twisted the fabric napkin in her hands before lowering her head.

"Truly? Izzy, I see death all around you."

I snorted a laugh. "Yeah, I live with a dead guy."

"I mean it," she whispered. "I'm not talking about Shane. What I'm trying to say is that I feel like trouble is coming for you. That body they found at your house, it's just the beginning. Someone is watching you, maybe right now. You aren't safe."

I gaped at her. "Seriously? I guess it must be Tuesday then."

She sat back, tossing her napkin on the table. "I know you don't believe me, but that doesn't make it untrue. I know what I know, and right now, I know my big sister is in big trouble."

"Okay," I agreed grumpily. "Say I believe you. Can you put a face to this mysterious danger? A name?"

"It doesn't happen like that. It's just feelings, impressions."

"Look, Heather, I know you're trying to help. But

vague warnings don't do me any good. My business, hell, *my life*, is dangerous. I appreciate you looking out for me, but unless you have something a little more solid, keep it to yourself, okay? I can't afford to be jumping at shadows."

She swallowed the last of the contents of her glass. "Fine. But like it or not, I'm home now, and I'm going to look after you and the rest of the family."

The idea of little Heather looking after anyone was so sad it was almost funny.

"Oh," she continued, "and don't be too hard on Duke today. He's a good guy."

I just gaped at her, mouth full of tuna.

After dinner, I drove over to the firehouse where Duke worked. I'd managed to get a vague schedule from Phoebe without sending up any red flags on her end, so I knew he was supposed to be on duty. How Heather had known about my plans still had me scratching my head. I'd just have to get used to her *psychic abilities*. That was, if the whole thing weren't totally insane.

The firemen had probably just gotten back from a call when I arrived because three men in jeans and fire department T-shirts were cleaning and re-stocking one of the fire engines.

"Excuse me," I said, poking my head around the door to where one man was hunched over the front seat.

He turned to me. "What can I do for you?"

He's cute, was my first thought. Dark, wavy hair and a solid, square jaw. *Was that a requirement?*

Then another man, this one short, with a weird, black mustache and thinning hair that smelled vaguely of chicken walked over, and I knew I had my answer.

"Um, I'm looking for Duke. Is he around?"

Mustache Guy answered, "He's upstairs. This way."

I gave Cute Guy a wistful half-wave and followed the other man up the stairs to some sort of apartment. Duke was sitting on a beige couch playing Xbox with another fireman.

"Duke, you got a visitor," Mustache Guy announced.

With a bright smile that dimmed just a fraction when he saw me, Duke turned my way. He tossed the controller to Mustache Guy and leapt over the back of the sofa, landing in front of me.

"Can we talk? Privately?" I asked in a low voice.

That didn't stop the two other guys from making the noise twelve-year-old boys made when someone was scolded by a teacher. Part snicker, part whistle.

"Sure," he said, stuffing his hands in his pockets.

He led the way to the kitchen, which was empty and impeccably clean. Even the chrome faucet shined. I was admittedly surprised. I expected more of a gross dorm-room feel from a bunch of guys.

"What can I do for you?" He propped a hip against the counter.

Where did I begin this conversation? I debated for a minute before deciding just to blurt it out. I was good at blurting. "Are you a werewolf?"

The uncomfortable smile fell from his face instantly. "What are you talking about?"

"Okay, so here it is. You know I'm a PI. My partner is a vamp. I recently ran into a *were* in town. I know they're pretty rare, but Heather is, sort of psychic or something, and she said you felt different, whatever the hell that means, so I did some digging and..." I took a breath. "I found an article about you. Bear attack, minus the bear? Kinda suspect. So I figured I'd just ask you."

I stood there, breathing hard after my mini-speech. His mouth was hanging open, but I couldn't read his expression.

"I... you... This is insane. What did you say to Phoebe about all of this?" he demanded finally.

"Nothing. Even if it's true, it's not my place to tell her anything."

"What?"

"Look, Duke. You seem like a decent guy. Phoebe digs you. Great. Whatever. I just want to make sure you aren't putting her in danger. I *know* some of the local *were* are working for the vamps, and I just—"

"Wait. Go back a step. What?"

Oh. He didn't know. *Interesting.*

"Yeah, so there's some kind of inter-species cooperation going on here in Charleston. No idea what or why. But I know that it's a dangerous gig, getting involved with those people. If you're in a position that puts my sister at risk..." I let that hang between us.

He shook his head slowly. "I moved here to get away from the pack lifestyle. No way would I jump into bed with the vampires. I can't imagine it."

I snorted—couldn't help it. "So, you're what, a lone wolf?"

He smirked. "Something like that. Look, the locals don't know about me, none of them. I'd like to keep it that way."

I shrugged. "I'm good with that, as long as you answer a few questions for me."

He looked at me suspiciously.

"Where do you spend your full moons?"

He frowned. *Weres* could often control the changes, at least after the new wore off, but they still ran a bit hotter during their cycle. A PMS-ing *were* was a dangerous creature.

"I go camping, far away from the general population."

"And your, uh, lineage?" I asked, feeling uncomfortably like my mother.

Being a *were* was usually from an infected bite, but two infected people could produce a full-blooded *were* child. They were crazy rare, crazy powerful, and according to Dad's notes, mostly just crazy. But the bottom line was the children of a full-blood *were* and a human were almost always born *weres*, at least for a few generations, until the gene sort of faded out. So if he was a full blood, or the child of a full blood, then my potential nieces and nephews were prone to the furry.

"I was infected."

I nodded. "I assume you plan on telling Phoebe?"

He frowned. "At some point."

Uh-huh.

"You have two weeks."

His head snapped up.

"Look. My sister doesn't do anything halfway. If she's committed herself to you, it's with everything she has. It's a rare thing, a person with that capacity for love and forgiveness. So if you aren't serious about her, cut her loose now. If you are serious, then tell her. She deserves to know the truth."

He nodded silently.

"Oh, and we never had this conversation. If she says to me in a week, 'Hey, sis, my boyfriend's a werewolf.' I say, 'Really? I had no idea.' Get it?"

"Got it. Thanks, I guess."

I tipped my head and left the kitchen, walking past the men playing *Mario Kart*, and headed back to the house, ready to tackle the next thing on my Impossible-Crap-To-Do list.

CHAPTER 12

The house was empty when I got home. No sign of Shane or, thankfully, any more *presents.*

It was just dark enough that I flipped on every light in the house as I went. Yes, between the previous night and Heather's cryptic warnings, I was quickly becoming an electric company's dream.

My tiny yet surprisingly expensive dinner hadn't taken the edge off my rumbling stomach, so I opened the fridge to rummage for leftovers. Settling on some day-old pizza, I nuked my plate and went to my office to eat as I searched. The machine was blinking again. I hit the playback button. It took me a second to place the voice.

"Ms. Stone, it was really nice talking to you the other night. I'm calling because our church is having a prayer meeting tonight at eleven. I saw what happened on the news last night, and I wanted to express my sympathy and invite you to join us. Pastor Marlowe and I both hope you can make it. See you then." *Beep.*

The voice belonged to Pastor Marlowe's right-hand man, David Pierce.

Well, there was no way I was going to subject myself to Marlowe again, but I did decide to do some more intense background checks on the good pastor. I watched a few videos of his anti-vampire sermons. Same old rhetoric, but delivered by a handsome, charismatic man of the faith. I could see why people were drawn to him. He reminded me of the old-fashioned snake oil salesmen, saying just what you wanted to hear while simultaneously promising the moon and making you very afraid not to buy what he was selling.

There were a few articles on his wife's death, and a few on his daughter Melanie's medical condition. His congregation had launched a huge fundraising campaign to earn the money he needed for her pricey treatments. Even so, the doctors weren't holding out much hope, the general opinion being that it was a miracle she'd made it this long.

A little after ten, Shane came home, alone thankfully. I got that he was seeing Mercy, and on some level, I could deal with that. But seriously? She made me want to redecorate in Holy Object Chic.

Shane peeked his head around the doorframe, holding a bag from Bubba Sly's deli out like bait.

"Hungry?" he asked.

I looked at my half-eaten, now-cold-again pizza for a split second before dumping it in the trash.

"Bring it on."

He vanished, reappearing again with two paper plates. Handing me a Philly cheese steak with a side of salt and vinegar chips on my plate, he dropped into his usual place beside me. Vamps didn't have to eat solid food, but they could. Their taste buds didn't react quite like a human's did, or so Shane said, but that just made experiencing food more enjoyable. It was like getting to try everything all over again for the first time.

"Whatchya doin?" he asked.

Sighing, I took a bite. I answered around my mouth-watering sandwich. "Trying to figure out this Marlowe guy." I wiped my mouth. "He's big bad, no question. But what was his connection to Lisa?"

"She a member of his congregation?"

I shook my head. "According to her sister, she went to St. Peters, downtown."

"So why was the husband going there?"

I shrugged. "Convenient? He was going there for treatment for his gambling problem."

"We ever come up with any debts for the husband?"

"Nope. No money missing that I can see, no weird debts, no loans. Clean."

Shane swallowed. "And I had no luck with the bookies. They'd never even heard of the guy. How many gamblers do you know with zero debt?"

"None. So who was the wife working off the debts to?"

It was his turn to shrug.

"It's just so sad," I said thoughtfully. "A seemingly nice, normal suburban soccer mom gets coerced into prostitution to save her husband's sorry ass."

"The question is—did the husband know what

she was up to?" Shane added.

It was a very good question.

"The number-one question is still—who was he in debt to that the *vamps* were letting her work off his markers? Must have owed the vamps themselves," I said, thinking out loud.

"Or one of their subsidiaries."

I looked at Shane and blinked. Robert Welch was a vampire hater, part of Marlowe's anti-vampire movement, so why would he owe money to the vamps unless it was through a middleman?

"Shane, I could kiss you." I smiled.

He leaned away. "Eww. Girl cooties."

Jumping out of my chair, I went to the file cabinet and pulled open the drawer labeled B. I removed a manila folder, took it back to my chair, and opened it. It contained a list of all known businesses run by, associated with, or owing money to the vampires. *Thank you, Dad.*

Unfortunately, it was a very thick folder.

Shane set his plate on the edge of the desk and motioned with his hands. "Here, give me half. It'll go faster if I help."

I handed him a small stack. "I'm not sure what I'm looking for."

"I'll let you know if anything jumps out at me."

Smiling, I took another bite of my cheese steak and dug into the papers. The next time I looked up, my neck and back had cramped and it was eleven-thirty.

I closed the folder, careful to mark my spot.

"I gotta go." I stretched, rolling my neck side to side as I stood up.

"I'm going too."

I looked at him flatly. "No, you are gonna stay here and keep looking. The note said *come alone*, remember?"

"And it was written by a possibly psychotic Vampire Mafia boss, remember?" he snapped back.

"It's *Xavier*. He's helped us this far. Besides, he's your soon-to-be undead boss."

"He's only helping because he's attracted to you," Shane retorted.

That stopped me for a moment, and then I laughed. "Whatever."

"I can smell it," Shane admitted with a low growl.

Now I stopped laughing. "You can smell what, *exactly*?"

"The testosterone. He oozes it when you're around."

"Hold up." I planted my hands on my hips. "Were you planning on sharing this information?"

"Why? You don't do vampires."

Shane's bitter tone felt like he'd slapped me across the face. He had never acted bitter since he'd turned, or even like he wanted to get back together. I always sort of thought he felt the same way I did. It wasn't about not loving each other, it was about the fact we had no future together.

I wasn't sure what to say, so I opted for an irritated rebuttal. "So, some mystery person leaves me a *drained body* on the porch, and you don't think to mention that the local head vamp has a crush on me? What the hell, Shane?"

He shook his head. "Wasn't Xavier. I'd have smelled him on it."

"Um, unless Xavier is smarter and older than you and had either a helper or is just that scary good at killing people." I snapped my fingers. "Oh wait, he is all of those things. I seriously can't believe you've been keeping this from me."

Whatever he was going to say died on his lips, and Shane hung his head in dejection. It was his sad, puppy face. *Damn it.* Well, I wasn't in the mood for it this time.

"I'm going. You're staying. Period." I grabbed my jacket.

"What if it *was* Xavier?"

"Well, let's hope he likes me enough not to kill me, tonight at least," I retorted with as much venom as I could muster and stormed out of the house.

I really hadn't planned to go to the meet without some sort of backup, not that I'd admit that to Shane. I had barely turned the first corner before I dialed Tyger.

"What?" His voice crackled through the car.

"Hey, it's Isabel."

He grunted and mumbled something to someone on his end that I couldn't quite make out. "What can I do for you?"

I bit my bottom lip. We'd only just balanced the scales between us. I wasn't too fond of going into favor-debt with him, but this was a sort of a special circumstance. By special circumstance, I meant, of course, that I was too stubborn to admit that Shane might be right, and I probably did need someone watching my back.

"How did the keystroke recorder work out for you?" I asked.

"Fine. Figured out who was skimming the cash."

I blew out a breath. "Oh, well, that's good."

Tone very cool, he asked, "You wanna tell me why you're really calling me at almost midnight?"

"I'm going to a meeting tonight. Might be shady. I could use a pair of eyes from a distance. Just in case. You busy?"

He took a long drag of what I assumed was a cigarette before asking, "What happened to your usual wingman, what's-his-name?"

"He's unavailable. You up for this or not?"

A long pause, more whispers. "Sure. Where and when?"

I gave him the address. "And, Patrick?"

"Yeah?"

I took a deep breath. "You didn't happen to leave a dead guy on my porch, did you?"

He laughed out loud. "Nope. What, did Brooks forget his keys?"

"No. This guy tried to kill me, and then ended up on my doorstep as a gift-wrapped corpse."

His next words chilled me. "Sounds like someone did you a favor."

"See you soon," I said after a quiet minute.

"Yep." *Click.*

I snapped my phone closed and tossed it on the empty seat next to me. Sometimes, Patrick scared the living shit out of me. Other times, it paid to have friends in all the wrong places.

I pulled in to the empty parking lot with one minute to spare. There was only one light. I drove under it and threw the car in park. Stepping out, I took a quick survey of my surroundings, unable to forget what Patrick had said.

The address Xavier gave me was just north of Truxtun Avenue, not far from Storehouse Row. The area was practically a ghost town that late. The only noise was the nearby sound of cars on the freeway.

I sat on the hood of the car, determined to wait only ten minutes before getting the hell out of there, and hoping that somewhere in the unseen darkness, Patrick had my back.

"You came." Xavier's deep voice cut through the silence, causing me to whip my head around.

He was approaching from behind, his expensive-looking loafers making no sound as he moved toward me, looking as human as I'd ever seen. He lacked his normal predatory gait, something I wondered if he did deliberately to put me at ease. If so, it wasn't working. If anything, the unexpected change in his demeanor had me on edge.

"Yeah. You passed me a note in study hall, remember?" I heaved a tired sigh. "It's late and I've had a really long day, so if we could skip the formalities, that'd be great."

Xavier closed in, uncomfortably close, actually grazing my legs as he passed, and sat on the hood beside me.

He flashed his devastating smile. "You have a knack for asking all the wrong questions. You are aware of that, aren't you?"

I shook my head. "Or all the right ones, if you're looking at it from my point of view."

"Touché. I asked you to meet me because I have a few things I'd like to talk to you about. Privately."

I frowned, confused. "I thought that was my

line."

He shrugged, and it just looked wrong on him, like he was wearing someone else's clothes. The thought made me look down from his face for the first time and really take a look at what he was wearing.

Dark blue jeans and a light blue, button-down shirt, the first two buttons undone and the sleeves rolled to just below the elbow. *Vampire casual?* I wondered. It wasn't that it didn't look good on him, it did, but it was strange seeing him like that. Was he playing at human, and if so, was it for my benefit? I shook my head.

"What do you want?"

He smirked, as if my question took just a heartbeat too long, and he'd guessed I was checking him out. Which I totally wasn't—sort of.

"Your investigation has put Shane in a delicate situation. His indoctrination into the Conclave is this weekend. I'd hate to see anything put that in jeopardy."

I opened my mouth to say something, not sure what exactly, but he held up his hand.

"Please, let me finish. Being outside the sphere of protection of the Conclave is dangerous. It isn't just being accepted by the Council, it's the only way he can be declared a legal member of our society. There are perks. I'm sure he's mentioned a few of them. There are also responsibilities, and overall, he becomes ours. A threat to one of us is a threat to all of us. With this new legislation being passed, any vampire not aligned with a registered Conclave is considered a rogue and can be put down on sight, by human hunter or vampire. That's the deal. To remain legal citizens in this country, we must police ourselves, and adhere to whatever justice the humans here demand."

"I understand. But as for the case, if you guys haven't done anything wrong, then there's no problem."

He tilted his head to the side. "Something tells me you have very different ideas of right and wrong than we do."

"Fair enough. But I'm not talking about some moral ambiguity here. I'm talking about a woman's life. A woman I know for sure was hooking for you."

"Only because I told you. If I hadn't shared that information, you would be exactly where the police have been for the better part of a year. Precisely nowhere."

I shifted, leaning away from him. I was trying to shoot him a look of exasperation but just then, an errant breeze blew through his dark brown hair, and I actually felt my IQ drop ten points.

Shaking it off, I retorted, "Why *did* you show me that file? You had to know it would lead to more questions than answers."

He nodded. "Only to show you that you weren't crusading for an innocent. Mrs. Welch was much less Mary and much more Magdalene than anyone knew."

"She was working for you to pay off her husband's gambling debts, wasn't she?"

"Not for me. I operate a handful of gentlemen's clubs, but would never stoop to anything as distasteful as prostitution." He said the word as if it were something he'd have to scrape off his shoe.

"But you know who does, I assume?"

"One of my dancers showed up for work a few weeks back looking like a human punching bag. After a fair amount of questioning, she admitted to whoring on the side. The madam was one of our upper-level executives named Marissa Duchamp."

"And?" I asked, motioning for him to continue.

"And Marissa was investigated and dealt with appropriately, according to our laws."

"Wait..." I slid off the car. "Are you saying that being a madam is against vampire law?"

He scoffed. "Of course not. If she'd brought the idea to us, she would probably be raking in money hand over fist. But as it was, she began her little business off the books, behind our backs. That simply isn't tolerated."

I put my hands on my hips, tucking them into my pants pockets.

"So, let me get this straight. It's okay to run a prostitution ring, but not to do it without permission?"

"Precisely."

I rolled my eyes. "Can I talk to this Marissa person?"

"Perhaps. If you own a Ouija Board."

I made an O with my mouth. That put a damper on things. "Wait, you questioned her, right?"

He nodded.

"Did she happen to mention where she got her girls? I guess I'm just trying to figure out what sort of deal she worked out with Lisa. I mean, how does the husband fit in to all this? How did Marissa end up picking up a gambling tab? Was she into anything else?"

Xavier shook his head. "I'm afraid not. I can't think of a single thing that would link her to any sort of gambling ring. It's the one thing we don't have the market on, if you'd believe that."

"Where did she work?"

"For our offices at Morris, King, and Deford."

Suddenly, the gears in my brain clicked into place. "That's where the husband works. Is there anything else you'd like to tell me?"

He cocked his head to the side quizzically. "There is nothing else I can tell you about this case. However, I admit I am looking forward to seeing you at the Conclave for Shane's initiation."

"That reminds me... you didn't happen to leave me a, um, gift the other day, did you?"

He smiled. "No. Should I have?"

I shook my head. Shane was getting punched in the stomach later for that. "Of course not. It's just, well, someone left me a, well, a body."

He snickered, sliding gracefully off the car and leaning uncomfortably close to me. "And you assume it was me? Why is that, I wonder?"

I took an involuntary step back. "It's just something Shane said, but he's an idiot so..." I let that hang between us.

Xavier moved again, brushing past me once more, the line of our bodies grazing for less than a heartbeat.

"Okay," I said finally as he stood beside me, leaning on my car. "What's with this?" I motioned to his entire body.

He looked down. "What?"

"You know what I mean. Why are you acting all human and friendly and stuff?

He folded his arms across his chest and smiled. "What makes you think it's an act?"

I looked up as I spoke. The sky was clear and away from the bright lights of the city, you could see the vast expanse of sky. I took a deep breath.

"Because I've seen it before. My father had an affair when I was fifteen. I don't think my parents ever knew I knew, but I did. I'd hear them fighting before we'd get up for breakfast. My mother got really good at pretending to be happy. I remember thinking that maybe if she weren't so good at pretending to be happy, she might actually be better at just being happy." I looked at Xavier. His brown-green eyes studied mine. "I think you're like that. You wear this mask so no one sees the real you. Maybe you've worn it for so long that you don't know how to really just be yourself anymore."

It was his turn to look up at the sky.

"You are disturbingly acute for a human, you know that?"

I laughed. I'd been told that many times in not nearly as nice ways.

"You are right. I came here tonight trying to make you comfortable. I thought this," he motioned to his clothes, "would help. But you have caught me."

"Why? I mean, why do you care if I'm comfortable or not?"

"Because, you remind me of something I lost many years past. You have this glow to you. You walk into a room, and you command it, not by your strength or power, but by your sheer determination to live. It's a rare quality for a human to have a fire inside them that burns so brightly. I find more and more that I'm blinded by you."

Xavier stepped forward and cupped his hand under my chin. Carefully, as if he were holding a piece of fine china, he grazed his thumb across my lower lip, making my heart flutter. He leaned down to kiss me, but I stopped him.

"Tell me something." I whispered as the gears in my brain turned, trying to make sense of what was happening.

"What do you want to know?"

I swallowed. "Tell me something about you. Something you've never told anyone."

"Why?" he asked, still inches from my face, still holding my chin in his hand.

"Because, I want to see you. Really see you. I need to know I can trust you."

He leaned forward, not kissing me, just rested his forehead on mine and closed his eyes.

"You would ask for the one thing I cannot give you."

"Why?" I breathed.

Temporarily speechless, I watched as he dropped his hand and smiled. Turning his back to me, he walked away slowly and waved over his shoulder, leaving me standing there, stupefied. He was moving at human speed, but with an otherworldly flow that gave away his true nature.

"I'll be seeing you, Isabel." He said my name like a breath, a whisper on the breeze.

Then he was gone. Not in a cool, Draculaturning-into-mist kind of way, but in the back of a large, black sedan that whipped in out of nowhere, scooped him up, and sped off, throwing loose gravel in its wake.

In the distance, the growl of a motorcycle gearing up let me know that Patrick had been watching my back. The noise spurted once and faded into the distance.

Slipping into my own car, I headed for home, confident that Xavier had been honest, and maybe even a little helpful, and knowing that whatever game he was playing with me, I was about to be in way over my head.

I had just pulled to a stop outside my house when my cell phone rang, air-raid siren tone. Without looking, I knew the call was coming from the police station. Never a good thing.

I stifled a yawn as I flipped open the receiver. "Hello."

"Hey, Isabel. I need a favor," Shane said.

I could tell by the strain in his voice that this favor would likely involve bailing him out of jail.

CHAPTER 13

"You were arrested for *what*?" I asked again in disbelief.

Shane sighed on the other end of the line. "Loitering. Are you gonna come get me or not?"

Part of me wanted to ask why he didn't just call his rich vamp girlfriend or soon-to-be boss man to bail him out, but I held back. Truth was, in some sick, co-dependent, Dr. Phil kind of way, I was glad he'd called me.

"Keep your panties on. I'm on my way. Just relax and try not to eat anybody," I quipped.

In the background, I could hear a male voice tell Shane his time was up.

"Isabel, just hurry, okay?" Nervous tension was thick in his voice.

I quickly put in a call to Craig Gentry, a bail bondsman who'd done some work for my dad in the past, and made a beeline for the precinct.

Shane was sitting on a wooden bench just outside the magistrate's office, a young, nervous-looking officer standing behind him with a massive shotgun probably loaded with wooden pellets. Not fatal to vamps unless it took out the heart, but certainly enough to do some serious damage.

The kid couldn't have been more than twenty-one, and judging by his general pallor and sweaty forehead, Shane was probably the first vamp he'd ever seen, much less been tasked to guard. Seeing me walk in, Shane slumped just a fraction, visibly relaxing. It was a very human gesture. One of the many things I'd miss about him when he grew into his new life.

I nodded, warning him with my eyes not to make any sudden movements that might spook the newbie.

Reggie was waiting for me at the desk, chatting with Matilda, the night desk officer. He'd obviously been called in from home. Still wearing his Superman pajama pants and a gray sweatshirt, he cradled a cup of coffee with one hand and smoothed down his unruly bed head with the other.

"Reggie," I called, turning his attention to me.

"Ah, Isabel. Good to see you."

"Same here." I thumbed behind me. "Mind sending Skippy over there to get some coffee or something before he accidentally shoots my partner?"

Reggie laughed, leaned forward, and called over. "Hey Weston, I got it from here."

The kid looked like he might argue, but then thought better of it and closed his mouth, walking away backwards, watching the back of Shane's head the whole way.

"Thanks. So what happened?"

"Looks like Shane was over at the Quick Mart down the road from your place about midnight. Clerk thought he was acting 'suspicious,' so he called in the black and whites. Shane gave them some lip, and they moved to detain him when he flashed fang."

"Did he put up any resistance?" I asked, knowing as soon as the words were out of my mouth that it was a stupid question. If he'd resisted either he, or more likely they, would be in body bags.

Reggie chuckled. "Nah. But he gave Weston a good scare."

"The store owner pressing charges?"

"I doubt it. He was pretty pissed to get called in the middle of the night and dragged down here. He and Detective Richards are looking over the security footage right now. If the clerk jumped the gun, then most likely Shane will be free to go."

I turned and looked over my shoulder at Shane, who sat there wearing his best innocent face, then turned back to the desk.

"Hey, Reggie, has anyone taken mug shots yet?"

"No. If he's cut loose, there'll be no need to book him." His eyebrow shot up as he noticed the wide, up-to-no-good grin spreading across my face.

"Cause the thing is, I could really use some photos for the Christmas cards." I smiled.

Finally catching on, he erupted with laughter.

"Why not? You go break the bad news to Shane. I'll meet you in the back." He pointed over his shoulder to the double doors and the magistrate's office beyond.

I walked over to the bench where Shane sat.

"Bad news, the owner might be pressing charges. Reggie said you have to go get your mug shot and fingerprints taken. But he said I could go with you at least."

Shane stared at me, his mask of innocence morphing into sheer panic, then fading to mild boredom and resignation.

"Fine," he huffed.

The clink of snapping metal echoed in the nearly empty hallway as he got to his feet before remembering he was handcuffed to the bench. He held up his hands. The links between the cuffs were broken in half. Shane shrugged, and I beckoned for him to follow me down the hall.

By the time Joyce, the lady in charge of taking mug shots, was finished, Shane knew he'd been set up. Reggie and I were rolling with laughter. At first, Shane was confused, but then he looked at the nameplate Reggie had made for him and saw that it read, 'Merry Christmas from Stone Private Investigations.'

Shane's momentary look of outrage made me pause, hoping he wouldn't do something stupid, but he quickly recovered himself. Tossing the plate on the counter by the camera, he shot me a dirty look. I shrugged and continued to giggle.

As it turned out, the store manager didn't press charges, so I was able to take Shane home with only a stern warning about back talking the police—and a promise that Reggie would e-mail me the mug shots.

By the time we got home, it was almost four AM. As tired as I was, I was also wound up, so I decided to relax with a bowl of ridiculously sugary cereal before heading off to bed. Shane was sitting next to me on the sofa when, without warning, he lurched off the couch and sprinted for the door.

"Hey!" I complained, picking crunch berries off my jammie shirt and dropping them back in the bowl.

A growl from the front door had me hastily setting the bowl on the table and rushing after Shane. It was pitch dark, so I flicked on the porch light. Shane was huddled over what looked like a fallen woman. He turned to look at me, fangs extended, eyes dilated. Lying on the ground at his feet was Miss Trudi Polk from the Gamblers Anonymous meeting, her unseeing eyes wide with terror, her throat shredded like raw meat.

Bile rose up in the back of my mouth. I raced down the hall, barely making it to the bathroom before heaving my cereal everywhere.

With shaky hands, I rinsed out my mouth and took a small jar of menthol rub from the medicine cabinet, smearing a glob of it onto a hand towel before returning to the porch. It wasn't the smell of decay that bothered me—it was the raw hamburger smell of a fresh body that made my stomach turn. *Maybe Heather was on to something with the whole vegetarian thing*, I thought miserably.

Shane had turned off the porch light and grabbed two flashlights instead. When he heard me coming, he shot me a look that didn't need words. A look that was full of concern and a silent offer to deal with the body so I wouldn't have to see it again. I shook my head, holding the towel in front of my nose, as I took a flashlight from him.

"Go call the cops," I said from behind the rag.

"You sure?" Shane asked, shining a beam of light to Trudi's chest where a big, white gift tag was taped, with my name on it, next to a large, red bow.

My stomach heaved again, but I was able to hold it down. Not going to chance opening my mouth, I nodded, and Shane stepped past me and inside. I knelt down beside Trudi. I probably should have gone inside, but it felt wrong to leave her there. This poor woman, whose only mistake in life had been meeting me, had died a horrible death only to be left on my porch like some sick offering.

It was like when a cat brought a dead bird to the door as a gift to its owner, I thought. There was rage, yes, but more something feral, instinctual about the whole thing. As if I were dealing with a child or a caveman. I sat there in the darkness, sniffing menthol and crying. Between the fear, the exhaustion, and the general feeling of not being safe in my own skin, I cried like the weak little damsel in distress I swore I'd never be.

I must have been in a state of semi-shock when the police came out. Reggie, now in his official blue uniform, took our statements in the kitchen as I made coffee. There'd be no sleeping this night, not for any of us.

"Isabel, can you think of anyone, anyone at all, who might be doing these things?" Reggie asked as he accepted the fresh black coffee I poured for him.

I shook my head. I knew Shane suspected Xavier, but it didn't make any sense. Xavier was many things, but crazy didn't seem to be one of them. He might send flowers, even candy, but he'd never send corpses. It was too déclassé for him. The only other people who stuck out to me were Charles Marlowe—who might be doing something like that to try to implicate the vampires—or Robert Welch, who might be trying to scare me off his trail. I gave Reggie both names.

"But, I don't know. It feels more, juvenile, you know?"

"This isn't a bag of flaming dog crap, Isabel," Shane chastised gently.

Reggie tucked his small notebook into his shirt pocket. "Normally, I'd recommend police protection, but Shane, if you'll stick close to her, I'll call that good enough."

Shane nodded, and the two men shook hands.

Trudi was bagged and carted off to the morgue. The police finally finished their search of the house, yard, and neighborhood and took off. My bones ached with physical and emotional exhaustion, but there was no way I was going to bed now. I opted for a super-hot shower.

When I opened the bathroom door, after using all the hot water, I ran into Shane. Literally. He had obviously been standing guard the whole time. I shoved my wet towel into his arms and pushed him backwards.

"Don't think this gives you license to stalk me, Fang-face."

"Oh, I think you have enough stalkers, don't you?" Shane quipped, tossing the towel at the back of my head. I maneuvered around him to my bedroom door and slammed it in his face.

"Wow. That's mature," he called from the hallway.

I stuck my tongue out at the door.

He laughed. "I saw that."

"Liar," I said, rolling my eyes. I turned and pulled a fresh pair of tan slacks and a white cotton top out of my closet. When I'd dressed and opened the door, he was still there. I nearly barreled into him again.

"Okay, seriously. Enough of that. It's creeping me out."

He followed me downstairs. "Isabel, you know what this means? Anyone you know, anyone you're close to, could be a target for this guy."

"I know. Reggie is gonna have patrol cars outside Mom's bakery and at the house. Sarah is already back in school, so she's safe at least. I'm also gonna put in a call to Duke, have him stick close to Phoebe for a while."

"What's Duke gonna do?" Shane snorted, and I cringed. I hadn't told him about Duke's unique situation and had promised not to do so.

"Just having him around and aware might deter anyone from trying anything. I hope," I added softly, the lie stabbing me in the gut. I hated lying to Shane even more than I hated crying.

After making a few calls and nibbling some dry toast, the only thing I felt comfortable eating on my weak stomach, I grabbed the car keys and headed for the door.

"Where are you going?"

"To pay a visit to Robert Welch's office. Why?"

"Because I'm going with you, stupid."

I shifted onto my heels. "That's a great plan. Let's take you to the office of a man who is not only a vamp hater, but also already pissed that we are even on this case—"

"And possibly a homicidal maniac," he added, folding his arms across his chest.

"Just another day at the office," I reminded him.

"Besides," he continued, ignoring my comment, "I need to stop by the tailor to pick up my outfit for tonight."

It took a full second for my brain to piece together the fact that tonight was Shane's welcome ceremony. The one I had agreed to take part in. I mentally kicked myself. How could I have forgotten? But then, I knew the answer to that. I'd blocked it out, like some kind of PTSD, which was a condition I'd probably have for real tomorrow.

With a huff, I turned on my heel and headed for the car, Shane close on my heels. We stopped by the tailor first, you know, just in case Shane was staked or something and the place closed before we could get out of the hospital.

Priorities.

His outfit was delivered in a jet-black box tied with a blood-red ribbon. I had no idea what was inside, but my mind was conjuring images of sweeping capes and frilly, white shirts.

The law office was nearly empty when we arrived. The foyer looked more like a Gothic library than any office I'd ever seen. Ceiling to floor bookshelves lined the walls, with thick volumes of modern and ancient-looking texts in a multitude of languages. Some shelves held knickknacks or photos in frames, but not many. At a round desk in the center of the room sat a beautiful black woman, her hair long, straight, and shining like silk.

Her smile was bright as she welcomed us. "How can I help you today?"

"Is Curtis Welch in?"

"No, I'm afraid he's gone home for the weekend."

I put on a brisk tone. "Well, we need to see someone about a woman who used to work here. Marissa Duchamp."

Her smile faltered, but only for a minute before she motioned for us to wait as she picked up the phone and hit a button. "Hold on, please."

I turned my back to her and whispered to Shane, "You getting any familiar smells from this place?"

He took a discreet but deep breath and shook his head. "Humans here. All of them. Some faint older vamp scent, but nothing recent."

I nodded.

"If you'll have a seat, someone will be with you shortly," the secretary informed us.

With mumbled thanks, we took seats in a pair of brown leather chairs near the bathrooms. We hadn't been waiting five minutes when a tall, elderly man dressed like a butler came out to greet us.

"I'm Leonard Deford. Pleased to meet you."

He shook my hand, and then Shane's before motioning for us to follow him down the long, narrow hallway to the office at the end. The room was large, done in various kinds of wood, from the desk and chairs to the floor to the lamps, and it reeked of pine cleaner, reminding me of the aerosol spray my mother used on her artificial Christmas tree every year.

"Thank you for meeting with us," I said politely as we took seats in the hard-back chairs. They were surprisingly comfortable for having no cushion.

"Of course. What can I help you with?"

"We're investigating the disappearance of Lisa Welch. I was told she was employed by Ms. Duchamp."

Deford sat back, folding his hands over his belly. "Mrs. Welch wasn't employed here, though her husband works in our accounting pool."

"Do you know if Marissa was doing any work, off the books?"

"Marissa was our liaison to the Conclave." Deford leaned toward me across the desk. "About twenty years ago, the firm fell on hard times. The Conclave, through one of their subsidiaries, invested heavily and brought the firm back from the brink of foreclosure. Of course, if we'd known then what they were, well, we may have looked for help elsewhere."

"You have a grudge against the vampires?" Shane asked gently.

"Oh, no, nothing like that," Leonard replied with a smile. *Genuine?* "But since then, we have had to keep a liaison on staff here. We've taken cases that were sent directly to us through the Conclave. Made deals on cases I'd have liked to see go to trial, that sort of thing. It's like having someone constantly looking over your shoulder and telling you what to do."

"I can understand how frustrating that must be," I offered.

He glanced at Shane. "Still, we are in business when many are not, so I have no place to complain."

He'd pegged Shane for a vamp and didn't want it getting out that he was disgruntled with the status quo.

I cleared my throat to get his attention back to me. "About Marissa, did you know her well?"

"Not at all." He snickered. "Other than her exotic taste in office furniture, that is. Everything was imported from Bavaria, you see. I think that's where she was from. She didn't associate with anyone here except on the occasional business matter, but even then, she mostly kept to herself. Just locked away in her office..." He trailed off.

"Can you tell me, Mr. Deford, does your office hold any company poker games, after hours?"

He shrugged. "We occasionally get together for a brandy after work, but that's about it. Though I did hear that some staff do a weekly card game. All harmless fun, I assure you."

"Could we see her office?" Shane asked abruptly, his tone edging from kindly to bossy. He was playing the Undead card.

"Of course." Deford stood. "I have a meeting in five minutes. Would it be terribly rude to ask you to show yourselves out when you're finished? Oh, and please don't remove anything. Her replacement will be here Monday and has left specific instructions that nothing is to be taken from the office until he arrives."

"Of course. And thank you so much for your time, Mr. Deford." I smiled and shook his hand again.

As we exited, he pointed down a different hallway to another office door.

Compared to Xavier's sparse, impeccably clean desk, Marissa's office was a pigsty. There was a sleek laptop on the desk, half covered in sticky notes. Papers overflowed from In and Out boxes, and shelves were filled with notebooks, files, and the random empty blood bag. Marissa, for her impeccable taste in furniture, was a slob.

"Great," I mumbled, not looking forward to digging through the mess, "So, at least we know the first link in the chain. Robert owed Marissa from these office card games. She offers to let Lisa work off the debts. Lisa agrees and ends up dead. We know the vamps killed Marissa, so who killed Lisa? Maybe one of her clients?"

The vamps were the obvious suspects, but if Xavier had admitted to taking out Marissa, why would he lie about killing Lisa?

"Dibs on the computer." Shane smiled, leaving me alone to fend for myself.

"Loser. So, if you were a file on a secret prostitution ring, where would you be?" I asked more to myself than Shane.

"Hidden?" he answered absently as he turned on the computer and started opening files.

"Thank you, Captain Obvious." I reached for the pile nearest to me. Case notes and copies of police files, but nothing to do with our case.

This was going to take forever, I whined internally.

"Okay, so nothing out in the open." I worked through the problem aloud as I moved around the office.

"Where do *you* hide stuff?"

I snorted. "Like I'm gonna tell you. Wait, the desk. All the way from Bavaria, right?"

I moved behind where Shane sat in a rolling chair and pushed him aside. Kneeling down, I crawled under the desk and lay down. Taped to the underside of the center drawer was a small, brass key.

"Bingo!" I pulled it from its hiding spot and. After I crawled out, I held it up to Shane.

"So cliché," he tisked.

"Right? Haven't they ever seen a James Bond movie, or at least an episode of *Law & Order?*"

"So what does it open?"

"I'm not sure." Looking around, I spotted a bookshelf in the far back corner of the room. There, half-hidden under a stack of papers, sat a small, black-and-gold box. I snatched it. Sure enough, there was a small lock in the front.

"You get so lucky sometimes," Shane groused, shutting off the computer.

"It's not my fault vampires are so obvious and uncreative."

"There's nothing on the computer. Just a few case files. No e-mail, nothing."

"Figures." I stuck the key in the box and turned it. The lock popped open immediately, revealing a tiny, red book nestled within in the gold lining.

"Little black book?"

I held it up. "Nope. Looks like red is the new black."

CHAPTER 14

We tried to put everything back as it was, even taping the key back to the underside of the desk. Everything, that was, except the small, red book I tucked in my back pocket.

"It's not going to matter," Shane said darkly. "The next vamp that walks into that room is going to know someone was in there."

I shrugged. "Nothing we can do about that."

We nodded to the secretary as we left the upscale office and made our way back to the car. My stomach growled the minute I got behind the wheel.

"You finally ready to eat something?"

"Yeah, nothing with milk though," I answered with a frown.

"Understood. Tacos?"

"Chinese?"

"Subs?"

"Pizza?"

I paused, considering my options. We looked at each other and said in unison, "Cheeseburgers."

I laughed, and a tension I hadn't known I was

carrying melted from my shoulders. I turned the key and looked over my shoulder to back out. Catching a glimpse of Shane's black box on the backseat made the tension quickly return.

We drove through and headed home to enjoy our bag of greasy burgers. Thankfully, there were no unexpected packages on the porch, so we went straight through to the kitchen to sit at the table. Just as I took a huge bite of my burger, the phone rang.

Shane grabbed the receiver and answered. "Stone PI." He listened to the voice on the other end, and then held out the phone. "It's for you. It's the station."

I frowned, swallowed, and took the receiver. "This is Isabel Stone."

"Ms. Stone, this is Detective Mertz. Can you tell me where you were last night at approximately midnight?"

"At a late business meeting."

Her tone sharpened. "Can you tell me who was present at that meeting?"

"What is this about, exactly?"

"I have a suspect here who claims he was with you at the time in question."

My mind reeled. Surely, it wasn't Xavier. Who else...?

"I was with Patrick Stevens. I was meeting a prospective client. He came along to look after me, what with all the things going on here." My answer was semi-honest, at least.

"I see. And you are certain that he was with you?"

"Absolutely." But I'd answered too quickly. I

hadn't actually seen Patrick that night. I'd heard a bike and assumed it was him, but what if it hadn't been? "Can you tell me what he was accused of?"

"Assault. Jarrod Decker, an employee at Mr. Stevens' motorcycle shop, was beaten up pretty badly last night. Thank you for your time," the detective said and hung up abruptly.

"What was that about?" Shane asked as I handed him back the phone, and he returned it to the hook.

"I may have just been set up as an alibi," I said with a frown.

Would my childhood friend have really beaten up the guy who was stealing money from him? Totally possible. Would he use me to set up an alibi? I wouldn't put it past him, honestly. Who was I kidding? I knew all too well what kind of person Patrick had become. Part of me wanted to call him, to yell at him for using me like that. But hadn't I used him as well? What had I been thinking going to him for help?

There was nothing I could do about it now, so I filed it away. I might make my share of mistakes, but I never made the same one twice.

To Shane's credit, he said nothing.

Determined to change the subject, I pulled the red book out of my pocket and set it on the table in front of me. Wiping my hands down my jeans first, I opened it and read the first page. Then the next. And the next. My queasy stomach returned.

"It's a log book. Girl's names and a list of their clients on each page. There must be fifty girls named in here."

"And the clients?" Shane asked.

"No names, just phone numbers. No more than six per girl." I kept flipping. "Ah, here we go, Lisa. Five phone numbers and a running total at the bottom. Cash earned, maybe?"

I handed the book to Shane.

"It's counting down from fifty thousand, but it never hits zero, it just stops, see?" He pointed to the numbers at the bottom.

Sure enough.

"So the debt wasn't paid?"

He shrugged and flipped a few more pages. "Looks that way."

"But she was still using the credit card."

"Maybe it was some kind of advance pay?"

I bit my bottom lip. "Maybe."

"What are you thinking?"

"Do you think your friend Richard can get a reverse directory on these numbers?"

"He might consider it beneath him, actually."

"Well, give him a call."

"What are you going to do?" Shane asked as I dumped the rest of my burger in the trash.

"I've gotta go do my hair. We have a party to go to in a few hours." I smiled half-heartedly and headed upstairs.

CHAPTER 15

I hadn't been prepared for a great many things that night. I hadn't been prepared for the limo that picked us up. I hadn't been prepared for the way Shane looked in his tux pants, white shirt, and shiny black vest—so much like I imagined he would have looked on our wedding day that it actually took my breath away when I saw him. I hadn't been prepared for the swarm of flashing cameras and paparazzi as we pulled up to the turn-of-the-century mansion that served as Conclave headquarters, or for the heaviness in the pit of my stomach. Even through all the glitz, I felt like I was being thrown in a pool full of sharks.

But mostly, I hadn't been prepared for the deep, driving loneliness growing inside me as the clock continued to tick, each tiny sound bringing me closer to losing Shane—to losing a part of myself.

The golden gown Mercy sent fit me perfectly, clinging in all the right places, flaring in others. The fabric was a delicate combination of satin and lace. Not exactly the sort of gown you got off the rack at a local department store. If I hadn't been so nervous, I might have felt like a princess. As it was, I just wanted not to vomit.

Initiation was a big deal in the new celebrity that was the sexy, vampire lifestyle. Thanks to a few million lame books about sparkly, sensitive vampires, they—while abhorred on one hand—were super glamorous on the other. And Shane was the story of the day.

We were ushered in quickly by a group of very tall, very wide doormen who shielded us, as much as possible, from the frenzy. Still, I had no doubt that my stupefied face stepping out of the limo holding Shane's hand would be fodder for the next day's Society page.

Inside, soft orchestral music played. I mistook it for a recording before I spotted the actual orchestra playing in the library. I guessed vampires spared no expense.

The knot in my stomach grew to basketball size as we were led upstairs to a small bedroom decorated much like an upscale hotel—generic and impeccably clean, in a pattern of black and white. The only actual color was in the green stem of a potted orchid on the nightstand. Then our guard-escort instructed us to wait there before he turned and left.

I looked at Shane and raised an eyebrow.

He shrugged in response to my unasked question. "I'm sure they just want to walk us through the ceremony."

I smoothed my dress and sat on the edge of the bed.

"That would be nice. I'd hate to mess up the secret handshake," I said, my tone dry.

The fact was, even though I'd agreed to this, I hated it. Down to the tips of my toes, I hated that Shane would be leaving. It was selfish, childish really, but there it was. I really wanted to be all mature and understanding, but I wasn't. The possibility that someday I might be was the only thing keeping me from resorting to crying and begging him to come home with me right then. But I wouldn't. I wouldn't ask him to come, not if I wasn't going to keep him.

And I knew I wasn't.

In silence, he sat on the edge of the bed across from me. I looked at him, hoping to see a trace of hesitation or fear, but it was the cool, calm face of the undead. It looked so wrong on him, and yet at the same time, kind of right, too.

"You look beautiful," he said finally.

I felt the blush creep into my cheeks, but before I could say anything, the door opened and Xavier, Mercy, and Xavier's second in command, a busty redhead named Ahnarra, glided in. Mercy rushed to Shane, who stood and caught her in a tight embrace.

I turned my attention to Xavier. "So, what's the drill?"

He leaned casually against the dresser. "The ceremony is called *Valde Vitualamen*, or in English, the Great Sacrifice. It's symbolic of vampires cutting their ties with the human world and embracing their destiny as immortals."

"In the old days," Mercy said with a giggle, "vampires would actually kill all their human family in the ceremony."

I swallowed, but I refused to let her rile me. "I assume that isn't how it's done anymore?"

Ahnarra shot Mercy a look that was clearly a 'shut up' before saying, "No, that isn't done anymore. It hasn't been done for centuries."

"You have nothing to fear, Isabel," Xavier added. "I swear, no harm will come to you this evening."

I nodded. Vamps were lots of things, but once they gave their word, it was law, especially coming from someone in Xavier's sphere of authority. They could lie, but they thought themselves much too civilized for it. Lying was degrading, in their opinions, or so Shane had told me. Ironic that murder was perfectly all right, but lying was frowned upon.

Stupid vampires and their stupid rules.

Ahnarra stepped forward and motioned for Shane and me to stand in front of her. Once we were in position, she withdrew a thick, red ribbon from the back of her tight, red dress.

"Raise your arms, please," she said gently.

We did. She proceeded to wind the ribbon around his right arm and my left, essentially tying us together.

She stepped back and Xavier stepped forward, handing Shane a large, golden dagger, which Shane tucked into his belt.

"I will call the ceremony to order, say a few words, and then our new initiates will be brought forward, one pair at a time," Xavier informed us. "We have three joining us tonight. You and Shane will go last in the procession."

Ahnarra continued the narrative, "Then Shane

will be joined to us via Mercy, who is standing in for his sire. He will be bound to her, and by doing so, to the Conclave."

Mercy leaned on Shane, smiling as she added, "Then, we have our reception."

"And I can leave?" No way was I sticking around any longer than I had to.

"Of course," Ahnarra said quickly. "We will have a car standing by to take you home."

Xavier stepped forward, forcing Mercy back. Taking Shane by both shoulders, he leaned in. It looked like a hug, but I could sense he was whispering something to Shane, but I had no idea what. Then he repeated the action with me.

"Please, before you go home tonight, I would like to speak with you," he whispered and drew back.

I nodded quickly, and the three of them turned to leave.

"I'll send someone when we're ready for you. Until then, please wait here," Ahnarra said solemnly, closing the door behind her.

I looked down at my arm where I was latched to Shane with blood-red silk. "So, what do we do now?"

He looked at me and smiled. "Wanna thumb wrestle?"

The ballroom was filled with people in elaborate Victorian costumes. I felt like I'd just interrupted the masquerade scene in a *Phantom of the Opera* production. A red carpet was rolled out, leading from the rear entry doors to a small stage where Xavier sat in a chair that looked way too much like a throne for my taste.

Xavier was flanked by Ahnarra on his left, and a man I couldn't place on his right. Ahnarra, of course, wore her stunning red dress. The man looked older than Xavier, which I knew was deceiving. Mid-fortyish when he died, he had closely shorn salt-and- pepper hair. A mustache of the same color framed his narrow lips and ended in a goatee.

The first initiate, a slender but stunning blond woman, had already gone through the ceremony when we entered the room. As I watched, the orchestra played a soft tune and the couple in front of us proceeded forward at a wedding march pace.

I shivered and dropped my gaze to the floor. Counting to ten slowly to calm my breathing, I fought back full-fledged panic. Memories of standing alone at the altar on my wedding day came flooding back, as did all the daydreams I'd had of the moment when Shane would walk me back down the aisle as his wife. I wanted to cry, scream, or do something. But I didn't. I just swallowed my emotions down. I'd cry later, I promised myself, but not here, not in front of these people.

The music stopped abruptly. Looking up again, I watched as the male vampire in front of us drew a shiny dagger like the one Xavier had given Shane and with one swift motion, he sliced through the red ribbon. The scraps fluttered to the floor like leaves on the breeze. The human beside him stepped back and a vampire stepped in, taking his place. Xavier stood from his throne and withdrew a black ribbon from his vest pocket.

"This is the tie that binds, one to another. It is

our brotherhood, our unity. With this, we are one." Xavier's voice rang out over the silent crowd. He leaned over and tied the two vampire's arms together. When he was done, he stood and announced to the crowd, "Welcome our new brother, Doctor Peter Chandler."

The applause roared like thunder through the room, shattering the stillness as the new vampire moved into the crowd to be welcomed him with handshakes and hugs. The human was led to a room off to the side.

Shane gently squeezed my hand but kept his eyes forward as the music began again.

Feeling like I might hyperventilate, I picked a spot on the wall behind Xavier and focused on it as hard as I could, trying to drown out everything else. A soft gasp beside me brought me back to reality. We'd stopped in front of the stage, but something was wrong. Shane's nostrils were flared, his body rigid with tension.

"What is it?" I whispered, though I was sure the whole room could hear. He gave me a barely noticeable shake of his head and drew the dagger.

Something was wrong. I could feel it as sure as I could feel the blood pounding in my ears, but I couldn't put my finger on what it was. My nerves were too frazzled. I was hot all over, breathing too hard and too fast.

Giving my hand one final squeeze, Shane tensed. I closed my eyes, part of me hoping he'd stop, drop the knife, and walk out of the ballroom with me.

But he didn't.

I didn't feel the knife cut the ribbon. After a

second, I opened my eyes, expecting to see the red trimming still connecting us, but it was gone. My heart fell. Xavier was watching me, his emotions unreadable on his stoic face. They were waiting for me to move. I glanced at Shane, who was staring ahead, ignoring me as if I wasn't even there. I took a shaky step back.

Mercy swooped into my spot, flashing a bright smile over her shoulder at me before turning to face Xavier, who stood and spoke.

I didn't hear the words this time. Turning away, I walked slowly back down the red carpet, this time alone, and out into the hallway. I must have stumbled because one of the guards grabbed me by the waist and lifted me into his arms. Behind me, I heard applause erupt in the ballroom, and the tears started flowing from my eyes. I only knew that the guard was taking me away because the noise in the ballroom grew more and more distant.

I wasn't as scared as I knew I should be at being carried off by a strange vampire. All I knew was he was taking me away from that sound, and that was all I wanted.

CHAPTER 16

The guard left me in some kind of office, which I assumed belonged to Xavier, with a bottle of water and a golden chenille blanket draped over my shoulders. As soon as I was alone, I could think again. I'd never had a panic attack before, but I could imagine that was what they felt like. I hated feeling out of control; it made me feel so weak. Using a bit of my water and the corner of the blanket, I carefully wiped the dark mascara stains from my face, praying that no one had witnessed my little meltdown. Especially Shane and Xavier. I hated the idea that Shane might feel sorry for me. I also hated the idea that Xavier might see me as a simpering, needy human.

My dad was a cop. The rule in the house when I was growing up was always, *Don't cry unless you're bleeding.* Sometimes not even then. The fact that I'd let my emotions get the better of me was equal parts disturbing and embarrassing.

No one would blame me, not after the week I'd had. *Fires, dead bodies, long-lost sisters, werewolves, and of course, all the vampire nonsense, were all contributing factors*, I told myself. It wasn't just Shane leaving that had shaken me. It was everything, my whole life. I'd held it all at bay for so long that at the first emotional crack in the wall, it had all come flooding out.

Swimming back to my full faculties, I took a long drink of water, tossed the blanket off, and rose to wander around the room. I admired the photographs on the walls. Some were in color but most were black and white or sepia.

The one that caught my eye above all the others was one of Xavier with, if I wasn't mistaken, Amelia Earhart. They were both dressed in 1940's aviator chic, complete with leather pilot's jackets and goggles, but what really struck me was the smile on his face. It was a real smile, the kind that lights up your eyes, the kind of smile that makes other people smile, too. The expression illuminated his already-handsome face.

I'd seen Xavier pretending to be human, but in the picture, all traces of his vampire nature were gone. I mean, if I didn't know he was much older than that, I might have thought from looking at the picture that he *was* human. It wasn't the uncomfortable fake-human act he'd put on for me. It was sincere. Honest. I wondered if he could still do that, let his guard down and just smile. I assumed it was something vamps lost with age, but maybe it wasn't. Maybe they had to be hard and cold because of the world they lived in, not because they lost the ability to do, to *be* anything else. Reaching out, I traced his image with my fingertip.

"That was the year I learned how to fly."

I jumped at Xavier interrupting my thoughts. "Oh, God," I yelped. "You can't sneak up on me like that!"

I turned to see him leaning against the doorjamb, legs crossed at the ankles, arms folded over his chest. His costume—*Did you still call it a costume if it'd been part of your wardrobe once?*—reminded me of a cross between a pirate and David Bowie in *Labyrinth*, all ruffles and golden embroidery. He looked hot with a capital H, but then, what else was new?

"So, you knew Amelia Earhart?" I asked pointing to the picture.

"I did. She was an amazing woman and a good friend."

"Do you know what really happened to her?" I asked jokingly.

His body tensed for a second, then relaxed again, but his tone was cold when he said, "She crashed and died."

Apparently, not a joking matter to him. In an effort to get my foot out of my mouth, I said, "I'm sorry you lost such a good friend."

He shrugged. "Such is the definition of a mortal life."

There wasn't much to say to that, so I just nodded.

Xavier reached out a hand as if to touch the frame, but he paused short. "You humans are so very fragile and so very unique, like snowflakes."

His voice was soft, uncurling in my head like a flower blossoming. Part of his vamp tricks, I figured.

Still, it was soothing, and that made it hard to care.

"Who's this?" I pointed to a more recent picture of Xavier standing beside a young man in a black graduation gown.

I wasn't trying to be nosy. Part of me just wanted to keep the conversation going in a direction away from work and death. Avoidance could be such a blessing sometimes.

"That is Devon Shannon, my last human relative. He graduated from MIT last spring."

"He's very handsome." I said, and I meant it. He looked a great deal like Xavier might have as a human.

"Yes, he takes after my sister, his great-great-great-great-grandmother. She would be proud."

"You seem proud, too."

Xavier nodded, looking away. "I am."

"So, is he going to be chosen?"

Xavier's eyes darkened. "No. No, he will live out his life as he's meant to."

I was two-for-two in the scraping a nerve department. "I'm sorry, I didn't mean to assume. It's just that I figured you'd be glad to have him as part of the Conclave family."

"Conclave is a family in many ways. But nothing can replace blood. You see, if Devon turns, my family line dies out."

I smiled to lighten the mood. "So are all vampires this big on family, or is it just you?"

"It is my one great regret. That I never had the opportunity to have a family, children of my own. You'd be amazed how things that seem to matter so little in the blush of youth can come to haunt you as time passes."

His voice was so sad, so haunted. I wanted to reach out, to comfort him in some small way, but I didn't know how. Some things you couldn't make better with pretty words and hugs. Some things you just had to accept and move on from.

"You wanted to talk to me?" I asked, breaking the uncomfortable silence that was quickly developing.

"I do. Please." He motioned to the chair across from the desk. Unlike his other office, this desk held only a stack of old books and a notepad with a pen tucked into the spiral coil binding it.

I sat, taking another sip of water, and waited for him to speak. He'd called this little meeting after all.

"I was born in Southern Louisiana in 1793. My father was a wealthy Spanish merchant, and my mother was his French mistress. After I was born, my father abandoned us. My mother took a job as a seamstress for another wealthy family and was quickly looked upon by the man of the house. My sister was born later that year. It was just the three of us for so long. We lived on scraps, whatever we could beg or steal. When I was fifteen, I took a job on a pirate ship captained by Jean Laffite. I always intended to go home after making my fortune on the high seas. But years passed and I grew selfish. I never forgot about them, I simply made excuse after excuse until..." He paused, his face distant as if lost in the memory. "One day, we were in port and I was a brazen youth of twenty-two by then. A beautiful woman glanced at me. She was obviously wealthy, her clothes were the finest, and her hair hung in rich, perfect, ebony curls. She invited me with her eyes the way only a woman can. I intended to bed her and rob her. What she had in mind for me was much worse. I became a vampire that night."

"Why are you telling me this?" I asked softly.

As he spoke, I could see the careful façade he'd built around himself begin to crack. His voice shook slightly, and his eyes were haunted, as if the ghosts of his past were hovering in front of him.

"You are a smart woman, Isabel," he began, resting his arms on the desk.

"Um, thanks?"

"And talented. And beautiful." He smiled, and I shifted uncomfortably in my seat. "I understand that Shane was your espoused, but now things are... platonic?"

I nodded, completely thrown off by where the conversation was headed.

"Yet tonight, he has joined us. I know that causes you some distress." He leaned forward. "So I must ask. Do you still love him?"

I let out the breath I'd been holding and laughed. "Yes, in some ways. I think I hate him a little, too," I added in all honesty. "But he's *important* to me."

"Important how?"

"Important enough that if you guys hadn't put Irena down after what she did, I would have. Important enough to kill for, to die for. He's..." I struggled for a way to make him understand "... family."

"Like a brother? Perhaps an uncle?" he asked, his voice dead serious.

It was enough to raise my hackles. "Okay, what's the deal?" I asked flatly, folding my hands in my lap.

"What does any of this matter? What's done is done."

"I ask because I wish to woo you."

"Woo what?" I asked, confused.

He sighed. "Woo. I would like to—how is it said now? Hook up." Xavier's eyebrows raised almost playfully, his face softened and hopeful with a half-smile.

I stood up so quickly that the chair fell over behind me. "Hold it right there. If you think there is any chance in hell of you and me having sex, you're crazy."

He stood up as well and walked toward me, every movement slow and deliberate. Flipping the strands of ebony hair from his face, he revealed his piercing, sky-blue eyes. His skin was pale and smooth, his lips pale pink and thin. His face was thin but chiseled, high cheekbones and one tiny dimple that I knew would appear only when he smiled. But he wasn't smiling now; he was looking at me with hungry desire from under his dark lashes.

"Why? Do you find me so repulsive?" He leaned in so our bodies were nearly touching. With one finger, he stroked my cheek, sending an army of shivers across my skin. He smelled like copper pennies and the night after a rainstorm. When he leaned forward slowly, gently pressing his lips against mine, I didn't stop him.

It had been a very long time since a man had touched me like that, and as if on instinct, my body rose to meet him. The blood rushed to my face, flushing me so hard I could feel it like flames on the tips of my ears. He slipped one hand behind me, his fingers splayed across the small of my back. The other hand moved down the line of my body, resting on my thigh for only a moment before traveling again.

I gasped, part in surprise, part in raw, consuming need. As of their own accord, my hands wandered too, one clutching the back of his neck, the other slowly caressing its way down his chest to the hard bulge of his pants.

All at once, I came back to myself, as if crashing back to earth after soaring above it for far too long. It was more embarrassment than physical pain, but the throbbing between my legs was deep and achy.

I took a step back and put my hands up, as if that simple, stupid, human gesture could hold him at bay. "I'm sorry, but this can't happen."

His face fell, like he'd never been rejected before, making me feel instantly guilty. "I mean, you're a good-looking guy, sure. But that doesn't mean I'm going to *hook up* with you."

"But you are emotionally compromised. Perhaps I could make you feel better."

He reached out and grazed my cheek with his fingers, which I promptly slapped away. Okay, maybe not *promptly*. I did have time to notice the cool, soft texture of his skin. Then I slapped his hand away.

"First of all, I'm not emotionally compromised, you dick," I said, fighting the urge to wipe my eyes to be sure I'd removed all traces of my earlier tears. "Second, that's not how it works. You don't just jump in the sack with someone because you think they're cute."

"Then how is it done?" he asked earnestly.

I shrugged. "You, you know, *woo*. You go to dinner and movies and get to know each other. It's called dating."

He raised an eyebrow. "That seems like a waste of time. I want you. I can see that you want me. I can hear your pulse speed up when you look at me—feel your body tense when I touch you. Why should we bother dating?"

"We don't date. I don't date vampires. Or sleep with them. Ever."

"Because you think we are monsters?" His question was a husky whisper.

"No. I knew I could never have a life with Shane after he was turned. Not because he was a monster, but because we were suddenly on two different paths. I had—have—a *plan* for my life. I wanted to be a teacher, to get married, raise a family. I wanted a husband, a partner I could grow old with. I wanted to watch my grandchildren play in Battery Park.

"I still want those things," I admitted, taking another step back.

It was my plan. Even though the first part hadn't worked out so well, it didn't mean I couldn't have the rest.

"I see. And those were things he could no longer give you."

"Exactly."

"But what does any of that have to do with sex?"

Although his voice was seductive again, it had less of an effect on me that time. I shook my head.

"I'm not one of those girls who just has sex with whoever. I want to be with someone I love, to give myself to someone I want to be with forever." I bit my lip as the last words left my mouth, but then continued quickly, "I'm sure there are lots of girls who'd be happy to have a roll in the hay with you." I pointed my thumb back toward my chest. "Just not this one."

Xavier took a step back and looked at me with his head tilted, like I'd just done a magic trick or something, and he was trying to figure it out. "Very well. I'm sorry if I offended you."

I waved it off. "It's fine. I'm going home now."

"But, I think I would still like to woo you. You are a most fascinating woman, Isabel." He lowers his voice to a dry whisper, "And you taste like strawberries and champagne."

I rolled my eyes. "Seriously, please don't. I have enough on my plate right now."

He smiled, the dimple appearing, "That's not a no."

I wasn't sure if I just didn't have the energy to correct him or if somewhere deep down, I liked the idea of being pursued by a good-looking guy, even if nothing would ever come of it.

Before I walked out the door, I added over my shoulder, "Look after Shane, okay?"

"I will," he promised.

Taking him at his word, I nodded and left the room. I hadn't made it as far as the front door before a scream and a crash drew me back to the ballroom. I kicked off my heels and ran full out, hiking up the hem of my gown as I moved.

The crowd had parted, and the music stopped. Mercy was screaming. Shane was lying on the floor, blood pouring out of his mouth as he heaved. The man who'd sat beside Xavier during the ceremony was standing over Shane, wiping a gouge in his neck with a handkerchief.

"What happened?" I screamed at Mercy.

Seeing me, her face twisted in rage. "This is your fault!" She pointed her finger in my face.

I skidded on my knees to a stop in front of Shane. He'd made it to all fours and was spitting blood onto the floor as his whole body convulsed.

Xavier must have come up behind me because I heard him demand, "Explain."

Ahnarra answered. "Sir, the neonate said something to Gerard about a dead human. Gerard told Shane to leave the detective to him, and Shane attacked him."

Even as he barked orders, Xavier grabbed me by the arm and pulled me up, tossing me like a rag doll to one of the guards. "Get Ms. Stone home. Clear out all the humans. Gerard, Ahnarra, Shane, to my office." I started to protest, but he turned to me. "This is a Conclave matter." Over his shoulder, he added, "And Mercy, clean this mess up."

"You promised to look after him," I reminded him quietly.

Mercy shot Xavier a look of shock, and then of insolence, but said nothing. I smiled over the shoulder of the guard who was carrying me toward the door. As I was being hauled off, I saw Shane rise to his feet, blood still dripping from his chin. He gave me a subtle nod, letting me know he was all right. For now at least.

This was what Shane wanted, I told myself. Mercy being put in her place was just a ray of sunshine on a cloudy day. Shane would be in deep trouble, that much I knew, and there was absolutely nothing I could do about it. He'd have to hold his own with his new 'family.' As much as I wanted to help, I knew I couldn't.

The guard put me down at the door, letting me walk to the car myself. A few flashbulbs went off, but they quickly recognized me as a mere human and turned their attention to the more exotic vampire guard. They shouted at him, everything from "How's the party?" to "How can you justify your existence?" Without Shane on my arm, I was no longer newsworthy.

I slid as gracefully as possible into the shiny, black stretch limo, the noise from the crowd outside going from a deafening roar to barely audible. Suddenly, it was my wedding day all over again. In that silent car, it felt like someone had punched a hole in my chest. I wasn't sure if it was just the emotions from that night or the devastation from that miserable day so long ago seeping back into my soul, but I'd never felt so alone in my entire life.

"Where to, Miss?" the driver asked, snapping me out of my pity party.

"Take me home."

CHAPTER 17

The house was completely dark when I walked in the door. I leaned back against the smooth wood, just letting myself breathe in and out. When I felt calm again, I flipped on the light switch, tossing my keys on the table and kicking off my shoes as I moved down the hallway toward the kitchen. I hit that switch and nearly jumped out of my skin.

"What the fu—?"

"Hey, sis," Heather said calmly, interrupting my expletive.

Phoebe smiled, dangling a DVD case from two fingers. "We brought tequila, ice cream, and *Dune*, the remake."

My little sisters were sitting at the marble-top table, each grinning like they had just lit the cat on fire or something.

Heather was wearing a light blue, spaghetti-strap dress with clouds on it. Her hair was pulled into symmetrical buns over each ear, peacock feather earrings dangling from each lobe. Phoebe had on a ratty David Bowie T-shirt and plaid pajama pants.

"What is it, sneak-up-on-Isabel day or something?" I complained, clutching my chest in mock surprise.

"We knew you'd be feeling down tonight. Figured we'd come have a sleepover, keep you company." Heather smiled and stood to make her way to the cabinets, where she started rummaging. "Let's make popcorn."

Phoebe slid out of her seat and gave me a hug, tequila bottle in hand, before jerking her head towards Heather. "At least we won't have to fight her for the worm."

I debated sending them back to Mom's. But, truth be told, I was really glad not to be alone.

"Aha!" Heather turned, holding a bag of microwave popcorn over her head.

I snatched it away, pulled off the wrapper, and tossed it in the microwave. Then I hugged her. "Thanks for being here."

"We're family. Family looks out for each other, right?"

"Right," Phoebe chimed in, retrieving some glasses from the dishwasher.

"So," I kicked off my shoes, "what kind of ice cream did you bring?"

Phoebe moved to the freezer. "What, do I look like an amateur?" She held up a pint of triple fudge brownie.

Heather grabbed three spoons.

"Hold on there, sis. Can you eat dairy? I mean, it comes from cows," I teased.

Heather brandished the spoons like weapons. "If you try to keep that ice cream away from me, I swear I'll poke you in the eye with this spoon."

Phoebe and I laughed at her serious face, then Phoebe poured a round into the shot glasses and handed them out.

"To family," she offered.

"To family," Heather and I said in unison.

Three glasses of tequila, a pint of ice cream, and two hours of *Dune* later, we were all warm and slurry. Like when we were children, I'd dragged all the blankets and pillows out, and we'd nested on the living room floor.

Heather was snoring softly as she lay snuggled on a tower of pillows.

"Izzy, can I ask you something serious?" Phoebe swallowed the last of the amber liquid in her glass.

"Oh, you can ask, but I might be too drunk to give you a serious answer."

She shifted onto her knees. "Okay. You and Shane, what happened? I mean, the whole story."

It was my turn to shift. "The bachelor party was just ending. Shane was drunk. He left the club alone, decided to walk back to the hotel to clear his head. He was attacked on the way. He never told me any specifics. Just that he saw a woman walking toward him, and then he woke up in the cage at the Conclave."

"And you, what? Gave up on him?"

I bristled. "No. I mean, I did what I could. He's here, or was here, living in my attic. What was I supposed to do?"

Phoebe set her empty glass on the table. "You

were supposed to stand by him. That's what you do when you love somebody, right? I mean, it was like you were all ready to marry him, then you just gave up on him. When he needed you to be there, you bailed."

"I did not bail on Shane," I protested, clutching a pillow. "I was there when he was locked in that cage, out of his mind with bloodlust. I was there when they let him out, when his parents shunned him, when the school fired him. I was there the whole time."

"But, you didn't love him anymore?" she asked, eyes sincere. "I'm not trying to pick at the scab; I really want to understand."

I sighed. "Of course I still loved him. I still do love him, in a way. But we don't have a future together anymore."

In a move I never saw coming, she smacked me upside the head with a pillow.

"Ow! What was that for?" I smacked her back.

"Because you're an idiot."

"Thanks for the support, sis," I snapped.

"I mean it, Izzy. Do you ever have that feeling like you just missed out on something that could have been amazing? That's what I see when I look at you and Shane. You two could be amazing. Epic."

"We could have been," I admitted.

"That's what I mean. It's not too late, you know. He's here. You're here. And really, he's worth it, isn't he? Isn't he worth the risk, Isabel?"

"You know, you're a morose drunk."

"At least I know enough that when something good walks into my life, I hold onto it with both hands. Where you are just a wuss."

I stared at my reflection in my now-empty glass, wondering when my little sister had gotten smarter than me.

When I opened my eyes, I had a crick in my neck, Heather and Phoebe were gone, and the clock read 1:13 PM. I dragged myself upstairs and into the shower after turning on the coffee pot, something I hadn't had to do for myself since the day Shane had moved in. Luckily for me, I didn't have a headache after the previous night's binge. However, I did replay Phoebe's words over and over in my head. I knew she was right. I just wasn't sure what to do about it. Besides, Shane had moved on, and with the Wicked Bitch of the East to boot.

I was just drying off when the phone rang. Remembering that I was alone in the house, I defiantly walked from the bathroom to my bedroom without putting on a robe.

"Hello. Stone Private Investigations. How can I help you?"

"Izzy, it's me." Shane's voice was casual, as if last night had never happened.

"What can I do for you, Shane?"

"I have some information for you."

"You can tell me when you come by to get your junk out of my attic." I smiled a little as I rubbed lotion onto my legs.

There was a shuffling sound, and then it was Xavier's voice on the phone.

"Please come by my office today. We have some things to discuss. Five o'clock."

The phone was shuffled again, and Shane was back on the line.

"You in trouble already?" I asked jokingly.

"You have no idea. See you at five."

I hung up the phone, curiosity going into overdrive. Shane had stumbled onto something during the ceremony, and I was betting whatever it was, it was bigger than I'd thought. Dressing quickly I headed downstairs to the smell of coffee brewing in the kitchen. It wasn't quite finished, but not patient enough to wait, I quickly swapped out the pot and my empty mug, the slow drip bubbling just a little as I made the transition.

I searched the cupboards for something to eat, coming up with only a half loaf of bread and some jelly. By the time I'd burnt my toast, the coffee cup was full and I quickly switched the pot back so it could finish filling.

My office was a mess, which wasn't typical. Of course, Shane had always been the one picking up behind me, so it did make sense. It also made my insides ache just a little. I'd had a lunch meeting on the books with a prospective client that day, so I called and rescheduled. I was simply too out of sorts to deal with anyone just yet. Then I spent the hours before the meet with Xavier pacing around the house, cleaning everything in sight, and going over the case file once more.

Cleaning helped me settle down and allowed my mind to focus on something other than the big, empty house. And it wasn't just a physical cleaning, I realized. It was an emotional one. The time had come to let go of all the crap that'd been weighing me down for so long. The wedding that wasn't, Dad's death, leaving school to take over the business—they had all been slowly eating away at me like a cancer. And I was done with all of them.

With a burst of inspiration, or perhaps insanity, I rearranged the living room and the office. It was something my mother did every so often, her way of feeling like she was in control even when other parts of her life were spinning wildly. I couldn't tell you how many times I'd woken up after a night that Dad was on stakeout to find the entire house had been reorganized, the furniture moved, and the photos on the walls rearranged.

By four o'clock, the place sparkled, everything was organized, and I was feeling much better. Realizing how grubby I'd become, thanks to dust bunnies the size of Shetland ponies hiding under the sofa, I decided to throw on some fresh clothes. I brushed out my hair, slipping into a pair of gray slacks and a black, vest-like top, and then examined myself in the mirror. With a final burst of vanity, I added the strand of pearls my mother had given me after my high school graduation. Not sure who I was dressing up for, I tossed my leather jacket over my shoulder and headed for the mansion.

CHAPTER 18

Unlike the night before, there were no cameramen crawling the gates. Security seemed lighter but much less discreet. I counted three guards patrolling the grounds, two at the gate, and another watching from the front door. I pulled my car into the circular driveway and parked. Leaning over, I flipped open my glove box to reveal the small handgun my father had given me. It was specially modified to fire wooden bullets. They wouldn't kill a vamp, but they would sure *deter* one. I slipped it inside the back of my waistband, pulling my jacket down over it as I got out.

Twilight was making the sky that ominous shade between red and purple as the sun sank low in the horizon. Before I was halfway up the steps, the bodyguard had pushed the wooden door open for me.

"Thanks," I muttered, following as he led me toward Xavier's office.

But staring at his massive back spurred my curiosity. The guy was well over six foot, all broad shoulders and chunky muscles. He wasn't overweight, but he had a build that on a human would have suggested a career as a pro-wrestler.

Envisioning some title like Mad Dog Muldoon or The Hitman, I just had to ask, "So, what's your name?"

He didn't slow down as he responded flatly, "Cage."

"Ah. I'm Isabel. It's nice to meet you, Cage."

He grunted. He was the same guard who'd carried me to Xavier's office the night before, the only witness to my meltdown. I was trying to be nice without having to come right out and thank him, but he remained aloof, so I dropped the small talk.

The corridor was longer than I remembered, the walls dotted with beautiful paintings and intricate sculptures in carved recesses. We passed a door that was cracked just a fraction, and I saw a bright light glowing. As someone moved inside, an odd-looking shadow passed the corner of my eye.

"What's in here?" I asked, my hand going to the doorknob.

In a heartbeat, Cage was there, his hand clutching mine. "Nothing for you to see. Come on."

I reluctantly let him lead me away.

We turned the corner and came upon Mercy leaning against the left-hand wall, scratching her nails on a stone sculpture that rested on a cylindrical pedestal. The way a cat scratched on furniture to sharpen its claws.

As soon as she caught sight of me, she pointed a finger my way and hissed, "You! This is all your fault."

"Really? Again? You should get some new material."

Without another word, she came at me like a rabid hyena. I thought for a moment that Cage would stop her, but she batted him aside as if he were a rag doll. Size, especially for vampires, was not indicative of strength. In a fraction of a second, I had the gun out and pulled the trigger.

The bullet caught her in the shoulder, the impact spinning her around. She managed to stay on her feet, and after a heartbeat, turned back to me again, expression wild as she lunged.

"I warned you once not to wound anything you couldn't kill," she spat.

I fired again, nailing her square in the throat. This time, the force of the bullet knocked her backwards, blood pouring down the front of her green silk blouse, turning it a macabre shade of brown.

I watched as she writhed on the floor, bubbles of blood erupting from the hole in her neck. Then right in front of my eyes, the hole shrank, knitting itself closed as the wooden pellet was expelled from her flesh.

There was a sound behind me and I spun, gun raised at chest level, and came face to face with Shane. He was wearing the remains of his tuxedo from the previous night.

I pointed to where the sleeves hung in tatters. "Good thing you bought that 'cause there's no way you'd be getting your deposit back."

He shrugged. With a sad smile, he put his hand

on top of my gun and gently pushed it down. "Better put it away."

Xavier, Ahnarra, and three others had joined us in the hallway. To be honest, I was so relieved to see Shane in one piece that I didn't care what else was going on. Realizing how fatal that mindset could potentially be, I smiled at him and turned my attention to Xavier as I slipped my gun back into my waistband.

"She started it," I stated as Xavier scowled at the woman bleeding all over his marble floor.

Climbing to his feet, Cage spoke up. "It's true. Mercy attacked her without warning and without provocation."

"Then it's a good thing Ms. Stone was able to protect herself." Xavier turned, glaring at Cage, who stood motionless. "I wonder, however, how it is that the human was able to come into my home armed. Surely, my guards would have thought to search her person?"

"Sir, she is just a human," Cage defended himself softly. "A small human at that."

"A small, pretty human with a weapon capable of causing serious harm to your master," Xavier retorted.

Cage bowed his head. "It will never happen again."

"Then clean this mess up and take Mercy downstairs. I will come soon to have a chat with her about how we treat our guests."

Mercy's eyes bulged, and she tried to say something in response, but nothing came out except a gurgle. In one smooth motion, Cage lifted her in a fireman's carry and took her down the hallway.

Seeming satisfied, Xavier turned to me. "Isabel, if you would follow me."

He headed toward his office. Shane was close behind me, with the other vampires not far off. Once inside, Xavier motioned for me to sit, but I shook my head. I wanted to be able to get to my gun if I needed to. Of course, if the situation deteriorated to the point where I needed to use it, I was pretty much dead anyway.

Xavier grinned like he could read my mind. "I'll let you keep your weapon since you've been so badly abused on this visit. However, I warn you, if you should ever return here, you'll not be allowed the same privilege."

I nodded. Shane sat in the empty chair, leaning forward with his elbows resting on his knees. He looked so tired, dark hair hanging shaggy around his face. His eyes, normally so beautifully blue, were rimmed in red.

He's hungry, I realized.

Xavier's words broke into my thoughts. "First, let me apologize for how you've been treated. Mercy is passionate, often beyond reason. Her behavior will be dealt with. Second, you are here because Shane has committed a quite terrible faux pas. I'll let him explain."

At a nod from Xavier, Shane spoke. "Last night, I was introduced to Gerard Von Swieten. It was his scent on Lisa's purse, in her car. I asked him why he was there, what he was doing. He told me to mind my own business. There was a fight."

Xavier interrupted, "Disputes between

vampires must be settled according to the rules of the Conclave. Outright aggression is forbidden. As a new member, Shane was ignorant of this rule. However, that does not excuse his actions."

Gerard stepped forward from the corner of the room. He wore a simple blue, button-down shirt tucked neatly into black slacks. His face was stern, hard. "And Shane will be punished, but that is not what we are here to discuss." He glanced at Xavier, a look that sent an involuntary shiver up my spine into the roots of my hair.

"Yes. Isabel, you are here because new evidence has come to my attention. It is a delicate matter, one we do not want taken to the police, if possible. You see, we are in a precarious situation. There are those who support our citizenship, but there are also those who work against us, those who would see us hunted like dogs in the streets. Revealing ourselves to the humans has laid down a gauntlet for us all. We refuse to hide any longer, but if we cannot be accepted by the humans, there are few options left to us. It would be war, you understand?"

I nodded. "I understand. But being part of the human world means respecting our laws. You can't just go around murdering people and expect to get away with it."

Xavier's dark eyes held mine as he spoke. "We, to the best of our ability, follow your laws. Do you know what Gerard's function in the Conclave is?"

I shook my head.

"Gerard is the Cleaner. When our world, our disputes, spill over into the human world, he cleans up the mess. He protects us as well as the humans."

"Then why did he kill Lisa Welch?" I demanded, knowing no answer he could give me would keep me from running straight to the cops as soon as they let me out of there.

"I did not kill the woman," Gerard answered. Seeing Xavier's motion to continue, Gerard explained. "I was investigating Marissa Du Champs. We believed she was running an unauthorized prostitution ring. I followed her on several occasions to an office space near the Old Slave Market. I discovered several human women on her payroll. She was using the women to extort several key political figures, moving them like chess pieces across the board. Only her agenda was not our own. She was using her influence to stir up anti-vampire sentiment. When she was questioned, she admitted that it was her goal to have the Conclave overthrown by the humans, so she could rise up and take control of it. She was quite insane by the end." He paused, frowning. "There was a woman, Lisa Welch, working for her. I followed Lisa one evening to find proof of Marissa's treachery and questioned her."

"By questioned, do you mean tortured?"

Neither my interruption nor my accusation fazed Gerard. "No. By this time, Marissa had been dealt with. I intended to take her place in the office, pretending to be the new liaison there. Actually," he paused, looking at Xavier, "I did feel that while her goals were skewed, the methods and results of Marissa's enterprise were quite useful. I still believe we should have kept the business. But alas."

He turned back to me. "She was panicked when

I confronted her. After some gentle persuasion, the woman admitted why she was working for Marissa. She told me her husband was in debt, and she had been brought in to pay off those debts. Only, one of her clients had threatened her. Threatened to expose her to her family."

"And what did you do?" I asked, not sure I wanted to hear the answer.

"I did as I was told. We dismantled the business, gave each of the women a hefty sum to purchase their silence, and erased any trace it had ever happened. Lisa's husband's debts were expunged, and I personally gave her enough money to make most men weep with gratitude."

Xavier sighed. "Only that wasn't the end. A few days later, some of the guards found Lisa's dead body on my doorstep."

"What? Why didn't you mention this before?" I almost screamed. Here I thought he'd been trying to help me, but Xavier was just covering his own ass.

"Because he didn't know," Gerard answered for him. "I was called upon, and I took care of the situation."

"Yes, and while Gerard performed his role as he is charged to do, in the future, I will be apprised of any such events," Xavier stated, an edge of warning in his voice.

"So what did you do with her?" I asked the gray-haired vampire.

"Her body was buried on the southern tip of Drum Island."

I sat down, my hands shaking. I'd known logically that Lisa Welch was dead. Statistically, the odds of finding her alive had always been minimal. But this, the callous tone of his voice as he calmly discussed burying her body, made my blood boil. It was all I could do to hold my tongue.

Shane put a hand on my knee and whispered, "Are you all right?"

I tilted my head, letting him see the anger in my face, and kept my eyes locked on his while I spoke to Gerard. "If you didn't kill her, then who did?"

"I'm sure I don't know. But for her to be left at our door in that way..."

He kept speaking, but I couldn't hear him anymore. My blood was pounding in my ears. I could see from the look on Shane's face that he just had the same thought I'd had.

"On your doorstep?" Shane asked.

Gerard nodded.

Shane looked at me. "You better tell them."

I laughed, "Why? It's not their problem. What are they gonna do about it?" I stood, anger lacing my voice. "He knew Lisa was being threatened, and it didn't even occur to him to try to help her. So why would he help me?"

"Is this about what you asked me?" Xavier's voice was calm and detached. "About someone leaving a body on your porch?"

"Bodies," I corrected. "And I'll deal with it. I don't need your help. Not that you'd give it anyway."

"I hope you understand why this information cannot be shared with the police," Xavier said carefully, like he was talking to a lion who'd just escaped its cage.

Crossing my arms over my chest, I faced off with

him. "I understand why you don't want the police to know. It'd look pretty bad for you, wouldn't it? Having a body show up at your doorstep, a woman who died hooking for you. But you know what? Her family deserves the truth."

I spun on my heel to walk out the door, but in a blink, Xavier was in front of me.

"The truth? About how she tried to save her husband's life by selling her body to pay off his debts? Yes, I'm sure that's exactly what her family wants to hear."

"You don't get it, do you?" I asked, steamed at his attitude and not about to hide it. "It doesn't matter what she did. She was their *family*. They deserve to know the truth because not knowing, always having that flicker of hope that someday she might walk through that door, those kids wondering why their mommy didn't love them enough to stay with them, it's living in hell, Xavier."

It was Shane's voice that pulled me back from the abyss.

"Isabel, we have to find out who killed her first. Then you can scream the truth from the rooftops if you need to, but like it or not, the Conclave didn't kill her. Someone did—someone who wanted the Conclave to take the blame for it. Don't you think that's a truth worth finding out?"

I sighed, relaxing my shoulders as I turned to look at him. "You're right. I'm going to find out who killed her."

"Even if it gets you killed too?" Shane asked, his voice tight.

I smiled bitterly. "No worries. Gerard is good

with a shovel. At least you'll know where to dig for me."

CHAPTER 19

I'd almost forgotten about Marissa's little red book until I arrived back at the office. The red light on my machine was blinking, so I hit play.

"Hey, Shane. It's Richard. Just wanted to let you know I got those names you asked for. Sent them to the e-mail you gave me. You owe me three pints of O-neg. Later." *Beep.*

Striping off my jacket I turned on the computer and checked my e-mail. Sure enough, there was a message from ladykillr74. I rolled my eyes. Vampires were so unoriginal. I clicked on it and brought up a list of names.

One name on that list was all I needed to see. Pastor Charles Marlowe. Pulling the phone from the cradle, I quickly dialed Shane's cell.

"Hello?" he answered on the first ring.

"I know who the killer is. We need to find some proof. Can you meet me at—?"

There was a click, and the line went dead. I glanced at the clock; it was a little after midnight. Hanging up the phone, I tried again. The line was still dead.

I rose from the desk chair, heading for the hallway where my purse hung when the cell inside it started to play the *Buffy* theme. I got two steps before the lights went out, plunging the house into total darkness. Taking another step, I tripped over the ottoman I'd just moved earlier that day. I scrambled to the wall and pulled myself up. For a second, I wondered if it were a power outage, then I realized the soft glow from the streetlight outside was coming through my blinds. The blood was pounding in my ears as I strained to listen for movement in the house. Even my quick, shallow breaths sounded so loud I felt like every one was a blinking light pointing to me, to where I hid in the darkness.

Mentally, I cursed myself for leaving my gun out in the glove box. That was when I heard it, a creak on the stairs. The sound of boots on wood, someone walking up from the basement. That was all I needed, a location. The basement access door was in the kitchen. If I hurried, I could make it to the front door before whomever it was made it up the stairs. I bolted, grabbing my purse as I ran by. As soon as my hand was on the doorknob, I felt a sharp pain in my back, and then a blast of electricity ripping through my body before everything went dark.

CHAPTER 20

I blinked. My first thought was, *Hey the lights are back on*, which just goes to show how hard I'd been hit. I shook my head to try to clear away the mental cobwebs. *Bad idea*. My ears rang like I had a cymbal player losing control in my brain. My arms ached, my back itched, and my legs were numb.

My mouth had been duct taped shut, my arms were taped behind my back at an awkward angle, and my legs were taped to my wheeled office chair, which explained the aching, itching, and numbness. Looking around as my senses slowly returned, I discovered I was in my kitchen. And I wasn't alone.

Why do I always wake up duct taped to something?

Sitting at my small table, flipping through an old photo album, was David Pierce, Pastor Marlowe's faithful lap dog.

He looked more like an IRS agent on a three-day bender than a serial killer. His hair was sandy colored and slicked back. His suit was clean but wrinkled, and his dark blue tie was askew. He wore black-framed glasses and a watch that either cost what I made in a year or was a really good knockoff. I rubbed my face on my shoulder, trying to pry up a corner of the tape. I knew if I could get the corner up and get it to stick to my shirt, I might be able to maneuver it at least partially off my mouth.

Hey, it wasn't my first rodeo.

He turned to me, his eyes drawn by the movement.

"Ah, good, you're awake. You know, you were a very pretty little girl, all smiles and curls." He stroked the photograph under his fingers.

I mumbled, "Keep your hands off my stuff," but what came out was, "Mmmmhmhmhm!"

The idea of this freak ogling my 'naked baby in the bathtub' pictures just pissed me off. I struggled against the tape holding me to the chair.

He smiled. "All right. I'll take the tape off, but you have to promise to be a good girl and not scream, okay?"

I nodded, blinking angry tears out of my eyes. He walked over and with one sharp tug, tore the tape off my face. It felt like he took my lips with it. *Hey, at least I could skip the waxing this week.*

I gasped from the pain, but also to fill my lungs for the scream I was working up. Before I made the sound, he had a butcher knife in his hand, the tip pressed just under my chin. I exhaled hard, but quietly.

I figured I'd try to put him at ease with a little small talk. "So, I admit, this is a surprise. I thought for sure it was your boss who was behind all this."

"See? I knew the first time we met that you were

a smart girl. Not much gets past you, does it? No, it's just me. For now, anyway."

I glanced toward the front door, and he followed my gaze.

"You're waiting for your partner to come save you. So am I. See, tonight, you're just the bait. I'm fishing for a bigger catch."

I bit down on my lip so hard that tears welled up in my eyes again. It was one thing for me to risk my own life, but the idea of this lunatic hurting Shane was almost more than I could stand. I took a deep breath, trying to focus as David continued talking.

"Don't look so distraught. You're important, too. So beautiful and smart. I'm going to save you, you know. Pastor and I, we're going to save everyone."

"From the vampires?" I asked, my voice cracking.

"Yes. And then, when everyone is safe, we can be together, you and me."

"You... you killed those people and left them on my door." It wasn't a question, but I was trying to process the situation, find a weakness.

"Yes, did you like them? They were gifts, you know," he added proudly. "I wanted you to feel safe. I read about that arsonist trying to kill you. And then he was out, a free man. I couldn't let him hurt you again."

I licked my lips. "And Trudi?"

"The bimbo? Yes. She was at the prayer meeting the other night. When you didn't show up, Pastor asked everyone to say a special prayer for you. She didn't like that at all. You should have heard the things she was saying afterward. Not very Christian."

"You were just protecting me," I said softly,

trying to both stall him and maybe convince him to release me.

"Did you know they were from me?" he asked, his eyes swimming with hope.

"Yes. I mean, I knew they were gifts. I knew they must be from someone... special."

He stepped back, smiling. My mind was reeling. I tested the restraints on my wrists, but the tape held tight. I started picking at it with my fingernails. I knew if I could just get a tear started, I could probably work myself free. But I had to buy myself some more time.

"Can you tell me about Lisa? Was she special too?" I asked.

"Lisa? No, she was a nobody. She had a chance to help the cause, but she refused. Can you believe that? Turned on her own kind. But even then, Pastor saw that she had a higher purpose to serve."

"Bringing down the vampires?" I asked. "Making people think they killed her?"

"They did kill her. They killed her soul, making her do those terrible things. Don't worry. She repented in the end. She was my first sacrificial lamb."

"And who is the last?"

He turned, frowning, but before he could answer, Shane blew into the house, his voice tight with bloodlust.

"Isabel!"

David looked down at me, but I shook my head. His smile fell once he realized I would not call Shane into that room. I'd chosen sides, and I wasn't on his.

He moved quickly, too quickly, inhumanly

quickly, and delivered one sharp backhand across my face. I felt the dull ache, and then the blood running down from my nose into my mouth. Closing my eyes, I spat, but the sour, coppery taste filled my mouth. When I opened my eyes, David was gone, but Shane knelt in front of me.

"Izzy, are you all right? Where did he—?"

A gun fired from behind him. Shane stood and turned. Reaching behind himself, he withdrew a small dart from his lower back. He had a minute to look at it quizzically before his face slackened.

I didn't have to wonder what it was. This time, I knew. Whatever article David had read about the incident with Billy Young must have included a tidbit about Shane being taken down with a dose of Ketamine. Silently, I swore to track down the author of the article and thoroughly kick his ass.

Shane dropped to the floor with a thud, unconscious. I screamed and flailed, trying to scoot the chair backwards to get to the drawers behind me, but with no luck. In a heartbeat, David was back. He leaned forward, kissing my forehead, before drawing back to hit me again.

When I woke up, I wasn't in a burning house, which was a minor improvement over the last time. I glanced around, taking in my surroundings. It was some kind of hospital, or at least it looked like the inside of a large hospital room. The walls were all heavy, white curtains on chains hanging from a slim track affixed to the tiled ceiling. The floor was generic beige linoleum with flecks of colored confetti inside. The only thing that was off was the smell. It didn't have the sterile, astringent odor of a hospital. It smelled musty and wet, like day-old laundry left in a washing machine.

I was taped to a metal folding chair, but I wasn't gagged, which was a small improvement. My legs were still numb, probably a side effect of having been taped so tightly to the chair legs, but aside from that and the throbbing pain in the side of my face, I was all right. Shane was another story.

He was chained to a gurney across the room, an IV dripping clear liquid into one arm while another IV drained blood from his other arm into a donation bag.

"Shane," I whispered. "Christ, Shane, wake up. Can you hear me?"

The white curtain pulled back, revealing Charles Marlowe in a set of green scrubs. "No, he can't hear you. He's heavily sedated."

"What do you want with us?" I struggled to keep my temper in check and my voice even.

It was one of those situations where having a chick tantrum might get me shot or at least gagged. Which was a shame because a tantrum might have felt really good right then.

"David, cut her loose, will you?"

From behind him, David obliged, using the butcher knife from my own kitchen to sever the tape holding me. I stared at it in his hand. Man, I was going to have to buy a new knife set now. No way was I slicing veggies with that again, *ever*. I wondered, a bit hysterically, if I could write that off as a business expense.

Immediately, blood rushed back into my legs, needling them with pain. It hurt like the devil, but it made me focus and pushed back the spiraling craziness that was leaking into my brain.

David took me by the arm and stood me up.

"Come here, I want to show you something," Marlowe said, leaving the room.

David pulled me along behind Marlowe. I glanced back over my shoulder at Shane, who lay deathly still. The sight might have frightened me more, but it was pretty much how he looked whenever he was sleeping. The only difference was the bright red tube lying against the pale flesh of his inner arm.

As it turned out, my sniffer was on the money. We weren't in a hospital at all; we were in some kind of converted basement that was sectioned off into clean rooms full of medical equipment.

"Does your flock know this is where their donations are going?" I snipped as we walked past a dirty room. The bed linens were balled up on the makeshift cot. The mattress and the sheets were stained dark brown with old blood. The smell caught me in the back of my throat and made me gag.

Marlowe turned to look at me and smiled before continuing forward, leading us into another room. He pulled the curtain back with a flourish, as if there was some sort of prize behind it. This room was much brighter, lit with beautiful standing lamps rather than overhead tubes. There was a table with a few vases of brightly colored flowers, daisies mostly, and framed photos. On the bed, tucked into frilly pink sheets, was a little girl, a bag of blood being fed intravenously into her small body. Her soft ringlets of hair spilled across the pillow like sea foam, her delicate mouth in a soft heart shape. Only her skin was pale, too pale, reminding me of Shane in the other room.

Marlowe rounded the bed, stroking the girl's white-blonde hair. "My daughter, Melanie. Isn't she beautiful?"

"I thought your daughter had Cystic Fibrosis," I stammered, stunned at the sight.

"She did, nearly died too. I had her brought here. You see, the Lord never closes a door without opening a window. Scientists have been using human stem cells to find a cure for these kinds of diseases, but that's barbaric, killing human embryos to use for science. But then, God gave us the answer. The vampires. They are monsters, yet their blood has amazing healing qualities. Just a few transfusions and she was breathing on her own, her paralysis cured, her brain damage reversed. A few more and she'll be awake again, walking around, a normal, healthy child. It's beautiful, God's plan."

I stared at him, slack jawed. "Aren't you afraid you'll turn her?"

"No, the first *donor* confided in me that the process for creation must be done a specific way to turn someone. And I have been quite careful, spacing out the transfusions, using different donors. You'll see. This will be the breakthrough science and medicine have been waiting for."

I actually felt my mouth drop open at his sincerity. He honestly thought this was the right thing to do.

"And you just took his word for it? I mean, I'm

no expert on where baby vamps come from, but I sure as shit wouldn't pump myself full of their blood and just hope for the best."

He snaps his fingers in my face. "The Lord will bless me for my efforts. He gave us this plague, and at first, I admit I didn't understand why. But then I saw it—the wisdom and glory in his plan! How could you disbelieve?"

"So we, what? Harvest the vampires like cattle? Won't that be hard? You know, 'cause of the fangs and all? Oh, plus, it's illegal."

"That's why they must not be allowed to become citizens. As animals, we can do with them as we please."

"They're no better than animals anyway," David chimed in.

I pulled away gently, pretending to be dizzy, and backed up against the counter in the rear of the room. For effect, I held one hand out in front of me. "Hold on, just hold on. I'm still... fuzzy in my head."

I made a show of taking deep breaths over and over even as I reached behind me to the countertop. In moments, I had carefully tucked a scalpel into my back pocket.

Straightening, I took a step forward. I had my ticket out of that madhouse, but first, I was going to get some answers. "What about Lisa Welch?"

"Poor Lisa. She was corrupted by those demons. I asked her to help me procure a new blood donor after the first one expired. This was in the early stages of my research, before I realized that a vampire could only lose so much blood before the decay process began, and she *refused*. She said the vampires had been kind to her, looked after her. Can you believe that? After she whored for them like that."

"She was whoring with you though, right? I mean, I found her client list. She saw you a dozen times in the last year of her life. So were you upset that she refused to help you, or were you upset that she wouldn't fuck you anymore once they let her out of her contract?" I demanded.

David glanced from me to Marlowe, looking for some sort of denial. All he got was an arrogant look of indignation from his devout leader.

Marlowe shrugged. "I didn't know the vampires ran the service until she admitted it to me. I called her to come over late one night, but she said that she'd paid her debt and the vampires were letting her go. I begged her to stay, but she refused. Said the only reason she ever let me touch her was so they wouldn't kill her husband. She called me evil, *me*! When all the while she was a harlot for the demons."

"So you had David take care of her." I looked Marlowe straight in the eye. "David was just trying to protect you, to look after you, and you lied to him and used him to get revenge on Lisa." Not that I bought that for a second, but if I could get David believing it, get him riled up, then maybe...

"I saw an opportunity for her to be useful, so I took it. David was my angel of vengeance."

I cringed at the depraved sincerity in his voice, turning my attention to David. "So David, does Pastor know about your dirty little secret?"

Marlowe glared at David. "What secret?"

222

"Oh come on, you must have noticed some of your blood supplies vanishing a little too quickly?" I made a 'glug, glug' gesture and pointed to David.

"That's ridiculous," David said, his expression taut.

"Really? Then how can you be so fast?" I folded my arms across my chest. "You dropped a dead body on my doorstep while I was at home, with a vampire bloodhound not five yards away from the porch, and managed to do it without getting caught. Pretty fast for a human, right?"

"Dead bodies? What is she talking about, David?"

David pointed to himself with his thumb. "I did it for her, to protect her. They were evil people. They deserved to die. And I wanted her to know that I could protect her, that she didn't need the vampire. She had me."

Marlowe moved forward and lashed out to slap David in the face. But in a blur of speed, David stepped backward out of range before the blow landed.

"It's true!" Marlowe bellowed.

"Liar!" David accused, lunging forward.

The men grappled with each other as I quickly slipped out of the door, booking it back to Shane's room.

Rushing to his bedside, I grabbed the IV of sedatives. With no time to be gentle, I tore the needle out of his arm, tape and all, and then leaned across his body to rip out the other needle. A spray of blood arced across the room. I used its tube to pull the donor bag up from the side of the bed where it hung, tossing it to the floor behind me. The bed's metal handrails then served as leverage for me to slide under the gurney in search of the lock holding Shane's chains together.

I cursed. It was a padlock. And I didn't have the key.

When a pair of men's shoes came into sight in the doorway, I froze under the gurney. Breath held, I wiggled forward on my back, trying to determine who'd won the fight. The shoes moved to the edge of the bed, and then turned away. I exhaled, sure whoever he was, he'd leave. An arm shot under the gurney and grabbed me by my hair, pulling me out. I screamed. No matter how tough you were, hair pulling was just painful.

Suddenly, I was face to face with David. His eyes were brown, but rimmed in red, the way a vampire's eyes looked when they were in the thrall of bloodlust. But it wasn't me he was looking at; it was the pool of blood beneath the IV bag I'd chucked onto the floor. It was slowly leaking a black-red puddle. My shoe had slid through the mess when David pulled me out, making a squeak that drew his attention downwards.

With one powerful push, he launched me across the room into the solid wall behind the curtains. I slammed into it at full force, my breath instantly pushed from my lungs, bouncing off to fall in a crumpled heap on the floor. Rolling onto my stomach, I looked over. David Pierce was on all fours, licking at the crimson puddle like a cat lapping up cream.

My stomach rolled at the grotesque sight. I'd seen junkies act the same way when they were whacked out on crystal, doing anything for another hit. And I knew that as soon as he wasn't distracted with that anymore, he'd turn on me and *I'd* be the puddle on the floor.

Reaching into my back pocket, I steeled my nerves. Shane might wake up soon, or he might not. Who knew how many or what kind of drugs they'd pumped into his system? Add that to the blood loss and he could be out for hours. I had to take my shot now, while David was distracted.

It was one of those moments where rational thought turned off and you were running on pure instinct. The adrenaline shot through my system like a comet, making everything clearer. Everything moved in slow motion, as if I were standing outside myself, watching events unfold but unable to control anything.

Gripping the scalpel tightly, I lunged, jumping onto David's back. He bucked wildly, but I held on with a tight chokehold. In a frightened haze, I drew the blade across his neck just under my arm, pushing the scalpel as deep and fast as I could. I clutched the now-slippery tool as I fell backwards off him, crab walking until I was a few paces away. Then I rolled into a crouch, readying myself to fight if he turned round.

But he didn't. Gasping for breath, David lurched, finally dropping face-first onto the floor, eyes open and glassy, the color in his irises fading from red back to brown.

With a sigh, I fell onto my butt, dropping the scalpel. It made a soft clink, but I hardly noticed due to the vomit crawling up my throat. I flipped over onto my hands and knees, retching all over the cool floor until nothing else would come up.

By the time I was done, the shaking had begun, tremors ripping their way up my spine and through my body. I tried to keep still, my muscles clenching around each quake, and I fought off the chill ravaging my body as shock began to settle in.

I heard footsteps thundering from somewhere seemingly far away, and within seconds, a small army of vampires, Xavier at the lead, were in the room with me, all looking ready for a fight.

I fell back onto my butt and laughed hysterically, my arms wrapped tightly around my middle. "You guys give new meaning to the phrase 'a day late and a dollar short,' you know that?"

CHAPTER 21

The vampires were helping rouse Shane, breaking through the heavy chains like they were made of paper instead of solid steel. Xavier put up his hand, wordlessly demanding silence. That was when I heard it—a small voice, its call echoing down the hallway. The sound made me feel like I had spiders crawling up my bare skin.

My breath caught in my throat. I put a hand on Xavier's arm. He frowned and raised his finger to his lips in a signal for me not to speak. Then he jerked his head in a "follow me" gesture. Together, we tracked the soft cries, Xavier in the lead. We stopped outside a door I recognized. Then Xavier moved quietly inside, and I followed close behind.

Melanie Marlowe was sitting upright in her bed. She'd pulled the tube of blood from her arm, the bag empty. Her cheeks were rosy, her hair the color of spun gold. She looked like a porcelain doll. Only the stillness gave her away.

No human child was so still.

Her eyes watched us like a vulture's, tracking

our every movement with frightening intensity. Her gaze swept over me, making me feel like a pig at a barbeque, before settling on Xavier.

Hands up in a gesture of peace, Xavier moved past me toward Melanie's bed. When he glanced down at the dead body of Charles Marlowe on the floor, she followed his gaze. Marlowe's head was turned at an impossible angle, almost backward, his eyes empty.

Melanie frowned. "Daddy?" she asked in her soft voice, bottom lip trembling.

Xavier quickly stepped over Marlowe, putting himself between the little girl and her father's corpse. He reminded me of a lion trainer in the circus. I just hoped he didn't do something stupid like stick his head in her mouth.

"It's okay, small one," he said in hushed tones as he sat on the bed beside her. "I'm not going to hurt you."

As if hypnotized by the child, he reached out to gently touch her hair. Heck, even from the doorway, I was hypnotized by her. It was sort of like watching a train wreck. You didn't want to look, but you just couldn't look away. I waited for her to strike out like a cobra and latch her baby fangs into Xavier. But if he was as tense as I was, it didn't show. He looked positively relaxed.

"Are you my daddy now?" she asked, smiling sweetly.

"If you want me to be," he answered, amused.

She lunged forward, her vampire speed blurring the motion. Before I could decide whether to make a move to protect him, I heard him laugh.

228

A short, happy sound. I looked closer and saw that she wasn't attacking him at all. She'd wrapped her slender arms around his neck in a hug.

"Daddy!" she exclaimed, voice full of joy like the sound of chimes on the breeze.

Xavier embraced her. I waited, waited for the tiny monster to turn on him, but she didn't. Xavier stood, taking her with him. Her tiny legs wrapped around his waist, her bare feet locking at the ankles. As he carried her to the door, I got a glimpse of just what Xavier had given up, and I understood for the first time with perfect clarity what it meant for him to find this little girl. A child without a father for a father without a child.

Xavier moved past without a word. Melanie's red-rimmed eyes stared back at me over his shoulder as he returned to where Shane had been strapped to the gurney.

I shivered, goose bumps breaking out along my skin.

CHAPTER 22

I was in full-blown shock when the paramedics arrived. I wasn't sure if the room had always been that cold and I hadn't noticed, but my teeth were clacking like an old-fashioned typewriter. I felt like I'd been dunked in an ice bath. No part of me could get warm, even after they draped me with two heavy wool blankets. My arms and legs were heavy, numb from the chill in my veins. I wasn't talking yet, though the police had started questioning me. It was like the words were caught in my throat. Only Reggie's promise to get my statement at the hospital got them to leave me alone.

Xavier and the other vampires had gone, at my request, long before anyone else had arrived. Less for me to have to explain, and they didn't want their names associated with this fiasco anyway. So I decided to just deal with it on my own. Plus, I couldn't stand Melanie's creepy little eyes staring at me from where she clung to Xavier like a monkey to a tree.

At first, all I could see was the blood. I mean, it

was everywhere, including all over me. It started to dry and itch. Finally, Reggie took pity on me and let me wash my hands and face in the upstairs sink. I felt a little more human after that, at least, until I saw what I'd done to David as they wheeled him out of the house. The vampire blood was still in his system, keeping him semi-alive, but for how long was anyone's guess. Even vampires would have a hard time surviving that much damage. From the looks of it, I'd almost taken his head completely off. The bile rose up in my stomach again. This time, there was nothing to puke up, so I just gagged.

Marlowe was dead. Broken neck, no big surprise. He'd gotten off lucky though. I mean, he never had to see his pretty little girl wake up fanged. In trying to save her life, he'd turned her into the thing he despised the most.

Irony, thou art a heartless bitch.

Xavier explained before he left that it was forbidden in Conclave law to create a vamp so young, and because she had no sire, he wasn't at all sure what to do with her. While most vamps woke up starving and mad with bloodlust, she'd just sat up in bed, looking like a tiny doll, and asked if Xavier would be her daddy, polite as could be. Xavier decided to take her back to the Conclave, and since I had no idea what else to do, I let him. I thought he saw something in her tiny face, something he'd been looking for, for a very long time. I thought he saw the opportunity for a family. A creepy, undead family though it might be.

I wasn't sure why exactly, but she scared me to the bone. If I were Xavier, I might have had to put her down as soon as I saw her. At the end of the day, I was glad it wasn't up to me, and I really hoped he knew what he was doing.

As Shane's punishment for breaking Conclave law when he attacked Gerard, he was assigned to be the Conclave liaison to the police department and lost his room in the mansion. I asked him if he felt like one of the Playboy Bunnies on her thirtieth birthday, and he smacked me with a throw pillow.

Yes, Shane was voted off Vampire Island. I didn't think either of us minded nearly as much as Xavier seemed to when Shane moved back into my attic. It was nice to have him back again, comfortable. But I couldn't help the nagging feeling that comfort came at the expense of something else.

Xavier became more persistent after that day in Marlowe's basement. I didn't know if it was something about seeing me covered in blood in full-on GI Jane mode that turned him on, and I wasn't sure I wanted to know, but he kept sending me flowers and asking me out to dinner. Every time something new came, I rolled my eyes and Shane smiled. On the plus side, the office smelled like roses and gardenias all the time now.

There were worse things.

Oh, and Phoebe confided in me that her boyfriend was a werewolf. She was much calmer about it than I would have been had our positions been reversed. I asked how she did it, and she told me that when you loved someone, nothing else mattered. Maybe she was right. Maybe I'd been holding on so tightly to my ideas of what I wanted my life to be that I'd forgotten to live it.

Maybe, I could have a fling with a vampire.
I mean, what could possibly go wrong?

Acknowledgements

This book began its life as a sort of experiment to see if I could write outside my traditional genre. Because I never intended it to be a real book, I drew heavily from my real family for inspiration, taking all the best parts of them and blowing them way out of proportion to create my cast of characters.

But in real life, my family is an eclectic mix of people who bring me the most joy and laughter a person could hope for in life. When we aren't wringing each other's necks, (and sometimes even when we are) we are the most tight-knit group of lunatics you have ever seen. So to them, I want to say thank you. You have each shaped me in different ways, and I wouldn't be the completely awesome person I am without you! (Though, one of you really should have taught me modesty—just sayin.')

And I would be remiss if I didn't also thank my publishing family over at Clean Teen Publishing. Everyone from the big bosses to the authors to the beta readers and street team peeps make it a joy to not only write books with them, but they also make the entire process feel like an adventure. You guys are my Hobbitises, for realsies. I look forward to many more quests with you!

I would also like to thank my writers group, the Tuesday Muses, for always letting me bounce crazy ideas around without judgment and for letting me play in their sandbox of wisdom. So, CJ, Rodney, Lisa, Aimee, Ann, and (the ghost of) Jay, you guys inspire me every week and I love you guys!

And last but never least, thank you, dear reader, for picking up this book and giving it a home. In the end, that's all that really matters.

XOXP
~S

ABOUT THE AUTHOR

A southern girl at heart, Ranae loves feeding people, gardening, and sweet tea. She hails from Oklahoma and lives with her family out west. She is the author of the Dark of Night novels from Crimson Tree Publishing.

Chasing Daybreak (2015)
Chasing Midnight (2015)
Chasing Dawn (2016)
Chasing Nightfall (2017)

Ranae Glass is the pen name for a popular YA author. She uses this name for her NA and adult novels.

https://www.facebook.com/ranaeglass

CPSIA information can be obtained at www.ICGtesting.com
Printed in the USA
LVOW12s0916170115

423243LV00004B/5/P